Cherokee Tears

Cherokee Tears

By
Ann Emmons Petri

Illustrated by
George Beale Emmons

iUniverse, Inc.
New York Lincoln Shanghai

Cherokee Tears

iUniverse, Inc.

For information address:
iUniverse, Inc.
2021 Pine Lake Road, Suite 100
Lincoln, NE 68512
www.iuniverse.com

ISBN: 0-595-31483-X

Printed in the United States of America

To the memory of
my sister Marianna
who, like the Cherokees,
struggled all of her life

CONTENTS

List of Illustrations

Acknowledgements

Brad Agnew, Professor of History, Northeastern State University of Oklahoma, who allowed me to use a map from his 1980 book on Fort Gibson.

Cynthia Bright, President of Bright Mountain Books, who provided me with much professional assistance.

Alice Emmons Burnish, my sister, who lovingly proofread and edited *Cherokee Tears.*

Jeny 'Running Brook' Covill, who allowed me to use the Cherokee Lord's Prayer.

George Ellison, a writer and naturalist residing in Bryson City, NC, who first told me about pot scrubbers.

George Beale Emmons, my brother, for his beautiful and inspiring illustrations for *Cherokee Tears.*

Dan Goldman, our son-in-law, for his technological help.

Lisa Henske, our daughter, who edited *Cherokee Tears* and also came up with many wonderful word usage suggestions.

Gary Moore, historian at Fort Gibson State Park, Oklahoma, who told me about the 1835 Fort Gibson map.

Bill Petri, Sr., my husband, who accompanied me on a month long Trail of Tears fact-gathering trip and also created two maps for *Cherokee Tears.*

David Petri, our grandson, who scanned all the illustrations and maps into *Cherokee Tears.*

Steven Petri, our son, who edited *Cherokee Tears* and also suggested excellent plot revisions.

Ellen Raphaeli, Professor of English, Alexandria Campus, Northern Virginia Community College, who first taught me the finer points of writing and then became my mentor.

Rachel Wiedel, iUniverse Associate, who has helped so much with the publishing process.

Prologue

The Cherokee Indians, along with the Creeks, the Choctaws, the Chickasaws, and the Seminoles were known as the Five Civilized Tribes of North America. In 1540, when the Spanish explorer, Hernando De Soto, first made contact with the Cherokees, their hunting grounds stretched over 40 million acres and included parts of what are now Alabama, Georgia, Kentucky, North Carolina, South Carolina, Tennessee, and Virginia.

The Cherokees have the distinction of being the first Native Americans with their own written language. Around 1821, a Cherokee named Sequoyah, also known as George Guess, devised an alphabet for the 86 distinct sounds in the Cherokee language so that his people could send and receive written messages using "talking leaves" like the white man.

The system was easy to learn and the Cherokees quickly adopted it. The people subsequently enjoyed one of the highest literary rates in the world and in 1828, established a universally respected weekly bilingual newspaper, *The Cherokee Phoenix*, also a Native American first.

By the early nineteenth century, most of the Cherokees were farmers and lived in log cabins. They were also council and clan leaders as well as teachers, shopkeepers, healers, craftsmen, athletes, and artists. Some Cherokees married white people, and most of the rest, willingly or unwillingly, adapted to fit in with the white man's lifestyle. A number of Cherokees, mainly cotton and tobacco farmers, became so successful that they were able to live in elaborate houses on large prosperous plantations. Some of them, like their white counterparts, engaged in slave ownership.

Over the years, however, the United States Government, through relentless encroachment and, sometimes, outright deception, gradually succeeded in reducing the Cherokee Nation to fewer than 10 million acres, about one-fourth its original size.

During all this time, the Cherokees, for the most part, continued in good faith to make every effort to get along with the white man and entered into treaty after treaty with the United States. All were broken. Still, they never gave up hope that their sovereignty as a separate nation would be respected and that the United States would leave them in peace.

Tragically, it was not to be. America was expanding rapidly, constantly in need of more territory, and the Cherokees' land was considered especially choice. It also did not help that, sometime between 1815 and 1820, gold was discovered on Cherokee land in Lumpkin County, Georgia, and a mini gold rush was on. The Cherokees had to go.

The states, especially Georgia, continued to pass more and more laws that deprived the Cherokees of their rights. In 1830, Georgia began holding land lotteries in which plots of Cherokee land were deeded over to white citizens. Also in 1830, the United States Government, under the leadership of President Andrew Jackson passed the Indian Removal Act, which stipulated that the Five Civilized Tribes were to emigrate to reservations west of the Arkansas River in what is now Oklahoma, where supposedly comparable land had been set aside for them.

The situation grew more and more desperate. The Cherokee leaders, with the help of Samuel Worcester, a white missionary, and others, pleaded their cause in the Federal courts. One case, *Worcester v. State of Georgia*, went all the way to the United States Supreme Court.

On March 3, 1832, Chief Justice John Marshall announced the Court's decision in this case. He stated that the Cherokee Nation was indeed a sovereign land, separate and distinct from the United States of America (although dependent on it). Individual states, such as Georgia, had no right to interfere.

However, the Court's decision in favor of the Cherokees was never enforced. President Jackson, already allied with those pushing for the expulsion of the Cherokees, chose to ignore the ruling. He is said to have declared, "John Marshall has made his decision, now let him enforce it."

In preparation for the Indian removal, the U.S Army built stockades in strategic locations throughout the Cherokee Nation, and, in May 1838, under the leadership of General Winfield Scott, the roundup began. The Cherokees were driven into the stockades where they were kept prisoner in deplorable conditions.

Those who survived this imprisonment were then marched over 800 miles through the states of Tennessee, Kentucky, Illinois, Missouri, and Arkansas to what is now Oklahoma. Over the summer and fall of 1838, and through the winter of 1839, approximately 17,000 Cherokees, poorly clothed, malnourished, and weakened by the stockade internment made this journey. They called it *Nunna-da-ul-tsun'y,* The Trail Where We Cried. As many as 8,000 Cherokees are known to have perished.

Not all the Cherokees, however, took part in this march. With the help of Will Thomas, a white self-taught lawyer who was adopted into the Nation as a child, about 600 Cherokees living in Quallatown, North Carolina were made legal residents of that state and could not be removed.

There was another very important group of Cherokees who did not go to Oklahoma. When the roundup began, approximately 600 Cherokees sought refuge in caves and other hiding places high up in the Great Smoky Mountains. Some were soon captured and others died of starvation and disease, but approximately 500 of these brave Cherokees are known to have survived.

Together with descendents of the residents of Quallatown, these people are known as the Eastern Band of Cherokees. Today there are over 12,000 Eastern Band members living on or near the Cherokee Indian Reservation in North Carolina.

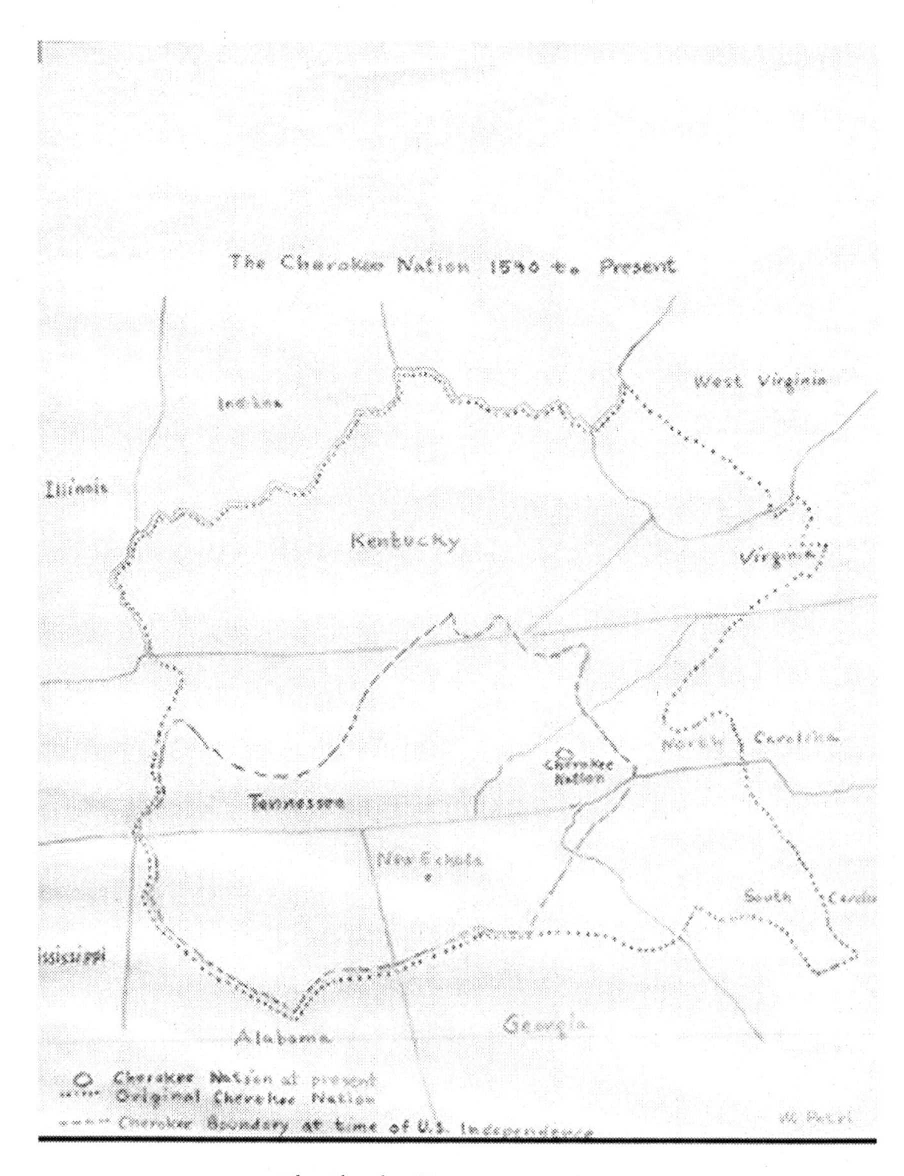

The Cherokee Nation 1570 to Present

Chapter 1

Gemini

New Echota, Georgia
(Capital of the Cherokee Nation)
May 1822

Taking the steps two at a time, the Georgia National Guardsman shouted through the doorway of the New Echota General Store to his comrades inside.

"Lame Bear's woman, that squaw Sweetwater, she's dropping her calf right now, in plain sight, over yonder by New Town Road."

Jumping down off the steps, he yelled back over his shoulder, "Ain't never seen nothin' like it! Come on ya'll!"

A small assortment of men, mostly recruits from the Georgia Militia, who were deployed in New Echota because of the ongoing dispute between the State of Georgia and the Cherokee Nation, were milling around three women huddled beside the road.

Avoiding eye contact with the bystanders already there, the newcomers elbowed their way to the front.

Sweetwater, her thick plaited dark hair already matted with sweat, was clutching her homespun linsey-woolsey skirt tightly around her pear-shaped middle and squatting down as if to pass water. Two older Cherokee women, Mattie Poor, Sweetwater's mother, and Halfmoon, a neighbor, were crouched on either side of her, each with a shoulder braced against her to provide support for the birthing position.

At home, Mattie Poor would have tied a loop of strong rope to a rafter of their cabin for Sweetwater to strain against. Then she and Lame Bear, Sweetwater's husband, would have respected her need for privacy by leaving her alone as much as possible to carry out this supreme accomplishment. But, instead, the three women had been caught far from their mountain homes on a basket-selling trip to New Echota.

In the late afternoon, after a long day spent sitting by the side of New Town Road in the Cherokee Capital selling their wagonload of intricate, double woven lightening baskets made over the winter, the three women started packing up for the long ride home even though they still had several left. Just before they pulled away, an itinerant peddler with a pushcart happened by and bought the last of their wares.

Tired but grateful to the old man, Mattie Poor, Halfmoon, and Sweetwater then started on the long bumpy ride to their homes in the foothills north of Ellijay, Georgia. They'd only just gotten a good start, however, when Sweetwater suddenly doubled over in agony.

"Something's wrong!" she cried. "The baby! I can feel it! Its head! It's right there, starting to come out. I can't hold it! It feels like it's coming right now. Oh no, no!"

Stopping the mule, Mattie Poor and Halfmoon helped Sweetwater out of the wagon and over to the side of the road, where her plight quickly turned into a spectacle for the curious young white soldiers. Thick ropes of dark red blood began to dribble in crooked rivulets down the insides of her pale thighs and then form sticky puddles on a pile of pine needles beneath her.

Every few minutes, a vise-like shuddering engulfed her entire body, followed by a lull during which she sagged against the shoulders of her companions. Just before the onset of the next spasm she would whimper in anticipation of the intense pain, and then fall silent, as the exertion of trying to expel the unrelenting bloody mass from her body became all consuming.

Before long, she began to fade in and out of consciousness and would have collapsed on the ground if not for Mattie Poor and Halfmoon's strong arms. Near the end of her seventh overwhelming convulsive effort, there was a hollow, sucking noise followed by a great gush of bloody birth water.

Two miniature heart-shaped fists no bigger than rose petals popped out of Sweetwater's body, and dangled languidly at the ends of tiny twig-like arms.

They hung there, swaying gently back and forth like shirtsleeves drying upside down on a clothesline.

As the soldiers watched, the fists slowly uncurled and the doll-size fingers splayed out into two perfect five-pointed stars. The translucent fingertips almost brushed the soft layer of pine needles on the ground. The men stared, transfixed.

"It's too soon," Sweetwater whispered to her mother between contractions. "At least two moons before my time."

Her voice became hoarse as she began to plead with her mother.

"Help me! Oh please, help me! Can't you do something? Maybe it's already dead. Do you think it's dead?"

Mattie Poor answered,

"Part of the baby is already birthed, Sweetwater, and it's alive. Hang on for just a little longer."

Seized again, Sweetwater strained with all her being. A glistening mass the size and color of a large ripe tomato bulged out. Then as the expulsion effort tapered off, it slipped back inside and disappeared, much like the snout of a cautious turtle.

Again and again, almost continuously now, Sweetwater bore down with all the strength she could summon, until, finally, the entire soggy, mucous covered head hung limply from the birth canal. And this time, it did not retreat back into its shell.

As the next contraction deepened, there was a collective, involuntary gasp from the crowd. There, on either side of the emerging baby's wet head, clinging snugly to the small hollow under each of its ears, they could now see two little feet attached to two bowed stick-like legs. Mattie Poor carefully cupped the slippery head in the palm of her hand as she separated the first baby from the feet and scrawny legs of what she now realized was another infant. Without looking up, she said calmly,

"I see two babes, Sweetwater, not just one. This first is alive and even trying to touch the ground with its little hands."

As she spoke, she carefully inserted the end of her index finger into the baby's mouth and cleaned it out.

"I can't tell yet whether the other one's quickened."

Then after leaning over and wiping her fingers on the grass, she firmly grasped the slippery little head by the cheekbones and waited for the next contraction. Patiently timing her efforts with Sweetwater's pushing, she twisted and pulled until she could free first one shoulder and then the other.

Soon the crowd could clearly see that two doll-like creatures were being squeezed out. The babies were clinging to each other in an inverted configuration like circus acrobats. Each was wrapped snugly round and round in the flattened glistening coils of its own brilliant blue umbilical cord.

As Mattie Poor became preoccupied with trying to hold and sort out one baby from the other, the head and then the arms of the second twin slid smoothly out of the birth canal. For just an instant during the final expulsion, this other baby, as it tumbled out into the world, stiffened its hands and fingers and spread them upwards to the heavens, perhaps beseeching the Great Spirit to let it stay a while longer among the stars and the Sky people.

Then, Mattie Poor gently lowered her precious load onto the ground. The two newborns lay there, in a squirming, worm-like heap, on top of their pine needle nest. Almost immediately, they were covered by spongy placental blankets, which gushed out after them along with a pulsating stream of warm bloody fluid.

With their voyeurism sated, the men seemed suddenly ashamed. Slowly, in groups of two or three, they began to mumble and avert their eyes. Backing up in embarrassment, they silently shuffled away.

All the while, they ignored the feeble mewings of the newborn twins as Mattie Poor and Halfmoon did their best to attend to them and to their exhausted, hemorrhaging mother.

CHAPTER 2

EBB TIDE

The foothills north of Ellijay, Georgia
Three days later

As he reached the one room log cabin northeast of the Land of Ridge and Valley in the far foothills of the Great Smoky Mountains, Lame Bear knew something was terribly wrong. He could feel the presence of the *Raven Mocker of Death* lurking nearby. He could almost smell him too.

Alarmed, he dropped the carcass of the young buck he was carrying on his shoulders and limped through the doorway. Mattie Poor was leaning over the rope and straw bed tamping fistfuls of dried moss between Sweetwater's legs. She was lying unnaturally still.

When he crossed over to her, he could see right away that her belly was flat. Piles of blood-soaked packing were strewn around on the dirt floor where Mattie Poor had hastily discarded them. As he drew near, he was careful to step over the debris. He did not want to crush any parts of the lost baby he was afraid lay there too.

Mattie Poor greeted him, saying,

"It is very bad, Lame Bear. Sweetwater's spirit is getting ready to leave. She has bled and bled. I don't know what to do anymore.

"It wasn't her birthing time, and yet she still managed to pass two perfect babies, a girl and boy. We were in New Echota with Halfmoon when it happened, and even though they were unready and very small, they're still alive." She gestured across the cabin to where Halfmoon was sitting by the fire.

"Over yonder," she said.

"It's been three days now and she just keeps bleeding," Mattie Poor said as she finished packing in the last of the moss.

"The ride back home in the wagon was hard on her. We tried to go slow, but still, every bump was painful for her and we were too long getting here."

As she bent over to pick up the used packing from the floor, her voice became muffled,

"Let me tell you one thing. It's a wonder those tiny babes are alive at all. But, you know, they're not out of the woods yet either.

"For two days now, Halfmoon and I've both been trying to get Sweetwater to drink comfrey tea. It's supposed to be good for bleeding but, so far, it hasn't done a thing. She just keeps bleeding and bleeding, and today, she's about slept the whole day away."

She stopped cleaning up for a moment and studied her daughter.

"We haven't been able to wake her even for sips of water since early this morning. I'm so glad you're home, Lame Bear. I was afraid she'd be gone before you got here."

Lame Bear propped his rifle in the corner and eased himself down on the edge of the bed. For a moment, he studied Sweetwater's face. Then he leaned over and placed his deeply lined, leathery cheek against her smooth one. He kissed her forehead and tasted the salt from her labor. Taking her limp hand in both of his big, gnarled ones, he cleared his throat and began speaking to her.

"You have paid me a great honor, Sweetwater. I'm so proud of you," he said quietly in his raspy voice.

"The Great Spirit has surely blessed us with these two living children. You have done well, and now you must stay here with us so that you can nourish our babes with your milk and bring them up in our ways."

Laying her hand back down by her side, he stood up and went over to the fireplace where Halfmoon was sitting on the bench taking care of the babies. After nodding at Halfmoon, he peered down into Sweetwater's double woven pie basket placed near a small bank of glowing embers. Even though the infants were partially covered with a burlap sack, he could see that they were sleeping face-to-face, with their foreheads touching and their arms and legs entwined.

He stood there for a moment, overcome by the wondrous sight, watching the rapid beating of their hearts against the delicate V-shaped indentations on the top of their downy heads. These two tiny beings seemed incredibly fragile and vulnerable to him but also very beautiful.

And, yet, mindful of his own deformities, he needed to make certain they were as perfect as they looked. Gently, he pulled back the burlap to inspect their limbs. He let out an audible sigh of relief when he saw the tangle of tiny but normal legs and feet.

He crossed over to the bed again.

"Our little unready ones are fine babes, Sweetwater. I never thought I'd be a father again, and, now, two at the same time."

As he often did, he rubbed his hand across his forehead and then spread his fingers to comb his thick black hair away from his eyes.

"But right now the old owl is calling. Hear him? He's telling us it's time to go down to the stream so that you can bathe in the cool evening water to stop your bleeding."

Mattie Poor stepped aside so that he could gather up Sweetwater's body. As he tried to lift her, however, something got in the way. She seemed unnaturally heavy. He glanced down to see if her legs were caught in the covers.

He saw, instead, that her buttocks were stuck fast to the blood soaked bedding. Mattie Poor stepped back in and pressed her palms against the stained straw mattress to hold it down so he could free her. As he lifted her, the pungent rust-like odor of blood escaped from the sodden bedclothes and entered his nostrils. The smell reminded him of the *Raven Mocker of Death* and made him afraid.

Angling his way around the bed and over to doorway, he ducked his head to pass under the lintel. He carried her down the worn dirt path to the place in the stream where she and Mattie Poor liked to do the washing. Picking his way carefully along the uneven sandy bank, he kicked off his moccasins and waded out to their special laundry rock. He inched down onto its hard flat surface and settled Sweetwater next to him with her head resting against his shoulder.

He heard her inhale sharply as the cold water flowed around her. Cradling her protectively against his chest, he used his other hand to clear away the dried blood clots and sticky clumps of moss clinging to her body.

She seemed more alert. In the twilight, he could see that her eyes were open. She was trying to focus on his face, and moving her lips as if to speak. Looking into her eyes, he used his strong fingers to begin to massage her abdomen.

"You must fight, Sweetwater, fight hard," he exhorted as he kissed the top of her head. Then he took in a deep breath and prepared to speak again. The effort was great because he was not used to so much talking.

"You can't leave me, you can't. You're my love, my Guide Star, my life," he said, his voice cracking. "Without you, I am nothing. Just a lonely old man with crooked feet.

"After the smallpox sickness took my first wife Callie and the two children, I was left with nothing. I started to wander the foothills and the mountains, half-drunk and out of my mind most of the time, not caring about hunting, trapping, or gathering food for the winter."

He continued kneading her stomach as he struggled to find words for his feelings.

"I thought there was nothing left for me after my family was taken from me, but I was wrong. When the snows began to fall, your mother, Mattie, and the other Beloved Women of the Wild Potato Clan, who had seen my suffering but respected my need to sorrow, wouldn't let me destroy myself. They took me in, giving me food and shelter all through that long hard winter.

"You were just a young girl then with beautiful eyes and a shy smile. I remember the first time I saw you. You brought me a basket of your mother's warm corncakes for my evening meal. Remember? And that, my dearest one, was the day I started to want to live again."

Sweetwater was shivering now but he could tell she was listening to him and her breathing was deeper and more vigorous.

"That spring, after I returned home and reclaimed my mother's farm, I found that I could not forget you. That's why I kept finding excuses to come back to your village every few months. I just wanted to see you again, to be near you.

"Even so, I never dreamed you would have me as your husband when you had your choice of all the fine young men in any of the other clans in your village. And who'd have thought that both you and your mother would be willing to leave your village and the Wild Potato Clan behind to move way out here to these lonely foothills with me. Not many women would do that, and especially not the cherished daughter of a Beloved Woman."

He broke off, "No, no, Sweetwater, don't close your eyes—keep looking at me—stay awake and fight, my love. Don't leave me. We've got so much to live for, and now, our new babes. They're so small and helpless," he said, "and they need names and so much else.

"Together we will teach them how to plant crops in the spring and then dry and lay in our stores for the winter, how to trap and fish, hunt and dress game, where to find the best grasses and reeds for baskets. All these things. I can't do it by myself, Sweetwater. You know I can't. I need you. Now, more than ever."

Lame Bear took her lifeless hand in his and cupped it protectively over his heart.

"Can you feel what you do to me?" he whispered.

"They say a woman marries to have a husband, a home of her own, and children, but a man marries only to plant his seed in the warm, dark place a woman hides under her skirt. That is surely part of it, true enough, but Sweetwater, my love, you have given me so much more.

"Don't leave me," he begged. "I can't stand to be alone again. Stay here with me, with Mattie, and with our babes. We need you so much. Oh please don't leave me just when we have so much more to live for.

"Fight Sweetwater, fight with all your strength. And I will do the same.

"Stay here, don't go," he implored. "Don't leave me all by myself again."

Until, finally, the clouds blurred the night sky and dimmed the light from the moon. He could just barely make out Mattie's silhouette against the shoreline.

All the while, the shadowy discharge continued to seep slowly and silently away from Sweetwater's body. It swirled around and around until the current captured it. Then it fanned out until all the water was sweetened.

CHAPTER 3

HETTIE AND SKY

Lame Bear's farm north of Ellijay, Georgia
May 1838 (sixteen years later)

"Anyway, how come you got all the good looks," Hettie said crossly to her twin Sky as they sat with their backs against the shady side of the corncrib.

Scraping the shriveled kernels off the last ears of corn left in the bottom of the raised floor of the shed was something Sky enjoyed doing and she knew he wouldn't be so apt to lose interest and wander off.

When each ear was scraped clean, he liked to sail the cob over the roof into the tinder pile in the other side of the shed. Hettie loved to hear him laugh as he did it. Especially now, because these days, there wasn't much left to laugh about.

"New Echota's full of talk that the soldiers are about ready to round up all us Cherokees and send us out west," Hettie said.

"Why, only last week when Mattie Poor had taken her to New Echota to buy supplies, soldiers had been standing around inside the General Store when they entered. She overheard them joking among themselves about moving the Cherokees out to the west and closing down the town.

"They acted like we weren't even there, talking about us any kind of way, not even bothering to move aside to let us pass," she added.

All but one, that is. A tall, slender National Guardsman with light brown hair, blue eyes and a long, thin face, was standing off by himself, and when she and

Mattie had entered the store, she remembered how he had stepped back politely to make room for them. Later, from the corner of her eye, she'd noticed him intently watching her, and a fleeting smile flickered across her face now as she recalled that incident.

She continued to carry on her one-sided conversation while she shucked the corn, acting as if Sky could hear every word.

"Why bother with all this fool work, anyway," she grumbled.

"All we're probably doing right now, with all the spring planting and the like, is laying in their stores for them. Just so those greedy white folks can take over our farms.

"Lame Bear and Mattie Poor both swear they'll never give up our land, no matter what," she said. "Me neither. Except those soldiers just keep coming and coming, taking and taking, and I don't see how we can stop them anymore. How do you think it'll all end, Sky? How?"

She sighed loudly and turned to study her twin who was absorbed in his task.

"There's no getting away from it," she thought. "It's true. He's as beautiful as I am plain. Mattie Poor says he looks just like our mother."

His unmarked face was long and thin with a straight nose. Thick, glossy hair hung down on his shoulders. Her hair was long too, but right now there were several uneven hanks around one ear because last week she'd tripped in a brier patch while out looking for early ripening raspberries and it had taken Mattie Poor the better part of an hour to cut out all the burrs.

Sky's skin was smooth and evenly bronzed by the bright springtime sun. Hers, on the other hand, was mottled with lighter spots of peeling skin on her nose and forehead in spite of wearing her sunbonnet most of the time, whenever she could remember it, that is. Rubbing that grease all over her face every night didn't seem to help much either.

Sky's deep-set eyes, light brown with flecks of green, were framed by thick black eyelashes and silky eyebrows. Hers were darker than his and right now they were smarting with the tears beginning to form at the memory of how that Wolf Clan girl at the missionary school had made fun of her, saying,

"Will you look at that! Why, your cheeks almost cover your eyes every time you laugh. You know that? How can you see like that, anyway?"

Unaware of her discontent, Sky concentrated on removing the withered kernels from the corncob. His soft full lips were parted ever so slightly, with the tip of his pink tongue caught gently between his evenly spaced white teeth.

He had just started wearing a turban like Lame Bear, not just for dress-up but for everyday too. However, it felt too hot for today and he had tossed it carelessly on the ground between them.

Hettie couldn't get used to the idea that Sky was ready for a turban and had grown taller than she, because no matter how big he got, she was afraid he'd never really be grown up. While other boys their age around New Echota were learning to hunt, fish, and plow, Sky was just beginning to be able to scrape corn and prime the pump.

"Why, he can't even wipe his own behind after doing his business out behind the cabin," she thought.

The trouble had begun long ago, the summer the twins were first learning to feed themselves and to walk. A terrible white man's sickness had spread throughout the whole valley. For days, Mattie Poor, Lame Bear, and the babies had lain on their straw mattresses in the darkened log cabin. Raging fevers turned the mottled rashes on their skin blood red. Their throats burned like hot coals and even the faint flickering of a candle had been too painful for their stricken eyes.

After many days, however, their bodies had cooled and their swallowing eased. Mattie Poor, Lame Bear, and Hettie slowly returned to good health.

But not Sky. Listless and unresponsive, he continued to sleep most of the time. Gradually, as the days wore on, Lame Bear and Mattie Poor realized that not only had he lost all his hearing, he had also forgotten how to walk and feed himself. Even worse, it seemed likely that he was going to remain childlike for the rest of his life.

"Still, there's no getting around it," Hettie said to herself, "he is beautiful."

She thought about the charcoal sketch hanging in the cabin over the bed she and Mattie Poor shared. The missionary's wife had sketched the twins on the last day of summer school. Sky was posed standing straight and tall like a proud soldier, with his arms locked at his sides. She was right next to him, but turned slightly away as if the sun was in her eyes. A scowl clouded her face.

"That Wolf Clan girl who teases me all the time is right," she thought to herself, "My cheeks are too fat and it's true, they do half cover my eyes."

She was jolted back to the present when Sky hit her on the head with a corncob.

"Ouch," she said, rubbing the spot. "That hurt."

He couldn't hear her, of course, but he sensed her annoyance and patted her arm in apology.

Hettie couldn't help smiling. It was hard to stay angry at Sky. Looking up, she checked the position of the sun and saw that it was just about time to start the long preparations for the evening meal. She got up and signaled for him to follow. They began to walk along the dirt trace that led up the hill towards the barn.

Beside the barn was an open slatted outbuilding and next to that was a small animal pen, which, this day, held a good-sized opossum. Lame Bear and Sky had caught it last week and brought it home in a burlap sack. Recently, Sky had started going with Lame Bear when he checked his line of traps, because it didn't matter how much noise he made. Hettie, though, was the one Lame Bear usually depended on now that he was starting to need help on his hunting and fishing trips. Mostly, Sky was just as happy to stay home with Mattie Poor, anyway.

The twins were fattening up the possum with the last few rotting winter apples left over in the bushel basket in the root cellar. The furry creature with the rat-like tail must have seen them coming because it was curled up in a motionless ball. Even so, Hettie could see that it was plump and ready to eat.

Sky picked up the stained club resting against the side of the pen as Hettie unfastened the latticework top. Taking careful aim at the pointed snout, he raised the club in the air and swung down as hard as he could. He squealed with delight as the blow was right on the mark.

Using the end of the club, he poked and prodded until he was sure there was no life. Then he reached down with his long fingers, lifted the possum by its hairless tail, and positioned it belly side up on the edge of the cage.

Then with the game knife Lame Bear kept in the barn, Hettie slit the possum from end to end. She wrapped the long tail around a wooden peg on the side of the barn, knotted it, and left the animal to drain nose down.

"May as well start on the rest of the chores," she said to herself and then signed, "Let's go," to Sky.

With Sky pumping, they filled a bucket with water for the mule, and together went to muck out his stall. They took turns forking the soiled straw into the wheelbarrow and toting it around back to the manure pit behind the barn.

Then, as usual, Hettie watched with amusement as Sky ladled out a scoop of dried corn from the covered feed bin and scattered it in a graceful arc for the range chickens. He loved to see them come running on their scrawny legs, but sometimes in the past, before she could stop him, he would get carried away and waste chicken feed. When Mattie Poor found out about it, Hettie got blamed. Now she paid more attention.

Back beside the animal pen, Hettie reached down and dried off her palms in the sandy soil. Solemnly, Sky did the same. Then, with quick, skillful movements, she eviscerated the possum, tossed its entrails into the hog pen, and handed the gutted animal to Sky. Side by side, they walked down the hill towards the cooking ring that stood in front of the weathered cabin.

Earlier in the afternoon, before Mattie Poor had left to go caning, she'd fixed the fire so that the heat from the coals would be just right at roasting time. She'd filled the black kettle with water and looped the handle onto the iron crane positioned over the fireplace. Now the water was bubbling ever so slightly above the glowing embers.

Taking the possum back from Sky, Hettie hooked Mattie Poor's long handled wooden cooking spoon into the gaping abdominal cavity. Balancing the body in the air like a tent draped over a pole, she carefully lowered it into the simmering water.

A short while later, she maneuvered the carcass over against the side of the pot and plucked a few hairs to see if the fur was ready for scraping. After several tries, a test hair finally pulled out easily. She fished the possum out with the bowl of the wooden spoon and plopped it on the long stone ledge next to the fireplace.

Sky had the scraper ready, and while she drizzled a bucket of water onto the skin to cool it, he began to rub the tool back and forth against the steaming fur.

"That's the way, Sky. Good work, good work!"

Even though the words were meaningless to him, he glowed in the reflection of pride on his sister's face and made soft, guttural, grunting sounds. While he continued working, she got up to measure out four helpings of cornmeal and some of Mattie Poor's dried peaches, which were sitting out next to the cornmeal softening in water. Using one of Mattie Poor's speckled blue enamel dishes, Hettie stirred the ingredients together, gradually adding more water until the mixture was soft and moist.

Then, with her arm cradling the chipped bowl, she waited until Sky was done scraping. When he finally finished, he rolled the possum over onto its back and held the cavity open so that she could stuff it. Using the spoon along with her hands, she packed the gritty sweet smelling stuffing into the gaping pocket.

One by one, she handed Sky the spines of dried holly leaves Mattie Poor kept in a tin cup on the porch. Even though he was slow and clumsy, with a little help from her every now and then, he eventually managed to push the sharp shafts through the skin to hold it together so she could bind it up with a length of honeysuckle.

Then Hettie carefully threaded the long iron roasting spit through the mouth of the naked and trussed possum. She gingerly probed inside along the underside of the backbone until the rod reached and passed through the hole where the anus had been.

She set it to roast over the fire and then they each picked up an empty water bucket and made their way to the well. There they took turns rinsing off the sticky possum residue from their arms and hands before filling the pails and carrying them back to the fireplace where they sat, periodically turning the handle of the spit so that the meat would roast evenly, and waited for their grandmother to come home.

Chapter 4

Bringing in the Cane

Lame Bear's farm
The same day

Mattie Poor spent most of the afternoon at her special canebrake by the river. A big and fine woman, with square shoulders and wide hips, she was taller than Lame Bear and heavy for a Cherokee. Her long hair, thin now and speckled with gray, was woven into a single wispy plait.

Sometimes she wore it wound around her head and fastened in the back with a wooden pin, but today she just let it hang over her shoulder.

Mattie Poor was fussy about her river cane. Only the longest and straightest would do. Especially now that she and Lame Bear had already laid in an ample supply of beautiful white oak from the North Slope. It was the finest she could remember. This winter she would be able to make quite a few of her famous double weave lightening baskets.

After she finished cutting and piling up the cane, she bound it all together into two bulky bales with long coils of honeysuckle vines she had sliced off for rope. Then she wrapped a rag around the blade of her knife and slipped it back into the deep pocket of her work apron.

Standing both bundles on end, she hoisted first one and then the other onto her thick shoulders. She balanced the load by trial and error, shrugging her shoulders and jiggling her hips.

With her arms encircling the bulky bales, she began a measured bobbing walk that relieved the burden at every other step. Concentrating on the rhythm of the up and down movements, she headed for home between the rows of last season's cornstalks and did not notice the two soldiers in the apple orchard ahead until she heard the nickering of their horses which were tethered there. She slowed down but otherwise did not acknowledge their presence. They were surveying the place again.

This was the farm for which she and Sweetwater had given up their own land to join with Lame Bear and now she considered it hers too. It was located in the last workable foothills before the rise of the *Unaka* Mountains, which the white people called the Great Smoky Mountains. Today, as usual, the mountains were wrapped in alternating layers of purple and white haze.

"Not that it matters anymore what they're doing," Mattie Poor thought to herself. "They've got us so worn down now we can't stop them even when they're breaking the law. Most of our land's already gone, and now Georgia's getting ready to steal what little we have left.

"Why, just last month, these same soldiers, well at least one of them, anyway, looks the same, had the nerve to march right into our cabin and, just like that, take Lame Bear's rifle. Yes sir. Just like that. Called it lawful confiscation, or some name like that, they did. And then they stood there, bold as can be, and told us our names are already on their relocation list."

She remembered back, some twenty years ago, when President Thomas Jefferson had advised her people that the best way to get along with the white man was to take on his ways.

"Let me tell you one thing," she said to herself. "We've done all that and where has it got us?

"We've learned to talk their language, and lots of Cherokees, even some women from the Wild Potato Clan, married up with them. And now, most all of us, we live in log houses just like them, and our men, they're mostly all farmers, too.

"And not so long ago, with the help of Sequoyah, that crazy old half-breed, we even got ourselves a set of talking leaves so we can send messages to each other from far away. Just like them. But none of it's done us any earthly good!"

She thought about how, over the years, the Council leaders had signed treaty after treaty, giving up more and more land, only to have the white men break their word every time. Nothing helped.

Now it was just a question of time, she knew, before the United States Army, backing up the State of Georgia, started removing the Cherokees from their land.

Everyone knew it was coming, although no one wanted to talk about it. And so Mattie Poor just kept on going, ignoring the two soldiers.

Meanwhile, Hettie and Sky were sitting by the fire minding the meat when they caught sight of their grandmother off in the distance, a lonely old figure so loaded down she looked like a pack mule.

Hettie immediately started complaining.

"Oh Lord, will you look at all that cane? You know she's going to make me quarter and strip every last stick. It oughta be enough that I watch over you, and do most all the chores besides, but it never is. Nothing satisfies her. Now I'll have to fuss with all that stupid cane.

"And, next winter, when the weather gets cold and we're back inside, she'll have me sitting at that wool wheel all day long, too, carding and spinning, carding and spinning, my hands all sore, same as last year. Just you wait and see."

But Sky was already halfway across the cornfield on his way to meet Mattie Poor. He stopped in his tracks, however, when he spotted the two men in their blue wool trousers and shiny leather boots. Making happy whooping noises, he veered off in their direction.

When Mattie Poor saw Sky break loose, she dropped her load and hurried over to cut him off, but she wasn't quick enough.

"That's the boy lives at Lame Bear's place." Sergeant Benjamin Stone, the taller of the two soldiers, said to Private Venable Guinnett, the new recruit who was working beside him.

"He's a deaf-mute and they say he's real slow, besides."

They stood there and watched the boy as he scampered across the field. A Georgia family named Campbell had won the right to purchase this parcel of land in the state lottery and the two soldiers were laying in the stakes for the final set of metes and bounds.

Benjamin's thick light brown hair was plastered to his forehead, and, as he straightened up to look at Sky running towards them, he tried to blink away the salty sweat that was stinging his blue eyes.

A quiet and polite young man, just turned twenty-one, Ben took his National Guard work very seriously and already had been rewarded with promotion to sergeant. He was determined to perform each new assignment to the best of his ability, and in spite of the hot sun, he really enjoyed surveying. He was fascinated with the instruments and he found the preciseness of the work very satisfying. Arithmetic had always been his best subject back in the one-room schoolhouse in Dalton, Georgia, his hometown.

"Can't hear a word you say." Benjamin said to his companion, as he took off his hat, got out his blue bandanna from his back pocket, and wiped the sweat from his clean-shaven face.

"Don't pay him no mind."

Venable Guinnett was grateful for the break. His arms ached from carrying the transit and all the other surveying equipment for the Sergeant and from digging all those holes.

Benjamin pointed across the field.

"Look over yonder—that's his grandma—coming to fetch him. She and his sister, her name's Hester but she goes by Hettie, take care of him 'cause his paw, Lame Bear, isn't much help. Drunk a lot of the time. Fact is, I saw him staggering around Ellijay just yesterday trying to trade his furs for whiskey."

Venable grew curious. "Where's the mother?"

"From what I understand, she passed on some time ago," Benjamin said. "There's only the four of them living on the place now, far as I know. Only those names on the relocation list, anyway."

Just then Sky reached Ben and joyously threw his arms around him.

"Say now, Boy, what you think you're doing?" Benjamin laughed as he only halfheartedly pushed the excited boy to one side.

Sky stood grinning and grunting as he looked from one soldier to the other. He was just reaching out his hand to finger the gleaming silver buckle on Benjamin's wide leather belt when Mattie Poor grabbed him from behind and roughly pushed him away. He turned to her and tried to hug her but she just punched him sharply in the chest, flicked her right fist towards her body twice, and pointed toward the cabin

As he reluctantly turned and began to make his way home, Sky kept looking back longingly at the surveyors. But Mattie Poor, who still had not said one single word, was marching right behind him, and each time he hesitated, she made the home sign again and, for good measure, gave him another shove.

Meanwhile, embarrassed by the actions of her grandmother, Hettie ran over to collect the cane bundles that Mattie Poor had left lying in the cornfield. She wasn't strong enough to load and carry them both on her shoulders, but she was able to balance one bale on her hip while she dragged the other behind her.

After only a few steps, however, the bundle she was pulling began to unravel. Squatting down, she gathered up the scattered stalks of cane and retied them as quickly as she could.

Venable Guinnett stood enjoying the spectacle of the dim-witted boy and the plight of his sister as she tried to retrieve the sticks of cane, but Benjamin Stone, upon seeing her predicament, immediately hurried over to help this young Cherokee who'd recently been catching his eye when he'd seen her around Ellijay and New Echota.

"Can I help you, Miss?" Benjamin called out, startling her, as he came up behind her.

"You sure look like you could use a hand," he said.

Shyly, she hung her head as the pungent odor of his sweat, mixed with the sweet smell of his nearly new leather boots, filled the air around her. She was surprised he knew her name but she recognized him immediately as the soldier she had noticed in the store. He was the one who had taken Lame Bear's rifle, too. She knew Mattie Poor would be angry if she spoke to him, and if she ignored him, maybe he'd move away and leave her be. Still, she couldn't stop herself from inhaling deeply to savor the heady masculine odors.

"Here, let me carry that," he said, reaching across her to pick up the first bundle of cane.

"I can take that one too, if you'll let me," he added, indicating the bundle she was struggling to lift off the ground.

She shook her head no as she tried to stand up and would have lost her balance if he hadn't reached out to steady her. The firm touch of his warm callused hand gripping her forearm caught her by surprise.

"Thank you," she finally managed to blurt out. She hoped he couldn't hear the pounding in her chest.

"I can manage by myself now," she stammered reaching for the bundle he was carrying. "Thank you for helping me."

"It's no trouble, Miss, really," Ben said, ignoring her outstretched hand, as he turned and started towards the cabin.

She followed him. The cane was scratching her side right through her clothing but she hardly noticed because she was so preoccupied with this young soldier striding along in front of her.

He was thin like Sky but his arms were more muscular and she noticed that he carried the bulky cane like it was nothing. His sweat soaked hair stuck out from under the sides and the back of his cap like porcupine quills, making her want to smile.

When he turned his head to check on her, she could see that his face was mottled from the sun just like hers.

"But his nose is long and thin," she thought. "Not spread all over his face like mine."

He slowed down so that she could catch up and walk beside him. Sensing her discomfort, he turned to her and said.

"I mean you no harm, Miss. I only want to help."

The visor of his cap hung low over his eyes, giving his face a serious, yet comical expression.

"Name's Stone, Benjamin Stone, and I hail from over in Dalton, but right now I'm stationed at Fort Wool in New Echota. You're Hester, Hettie. Right? I was at your house once, and I've also seen you around Ellijay and New Echota," he added.

She couldn't get any words out in response which was just as well because, looking up, she saw her grandmother, hands on hips, blocking the path just ahead of them.

Mattie Poor took a step toward Benjamin and drew herself up until they were standing almost shoulder-to-shoulder. Looking him over disdainfully, she held out her arms.

"I'll take that now," she said, coldly.

"Yes, Ma'am," he answered, without arguing, as he passed over the cane to her. He dusted the chaff off his hands and then brushed off the front of his uniform blouse.

Finally, just before he turned to go back to where Venable Guinnett was waiting, he took a long look at Hettie. Tipping his cap, he said,

"Goodbye Miss, good luck to you."

Walking behind her grandmother, with the load of cane scrunched against her hip, Hettie tried to calm herself. She did not understand what was causing her to feel so flustered.

"He isn't that good looking," she thought to herself, "and, besides, he's not even Cherokee."

But, still, her heart echoed in her ears and she felt light-headed and unsteady. No matter how carefully she tried to breathe, she couldn't seem to take in enough air to fill her lungs.

And just before she reached the barn, she turned around and felt her heart turn over when she saw him looking at her too.

Gemini

Stopping the mule, Mattie Poor and Halfmoon helped Sweetwater out of the wagon and over to the side of the road, where her plight quickly turned into a spectacle for the curious white soldiers.

Chapter 5

Now The Day Is Over

Lame Bear's farm
Later the same day

When she entered the cabin just before dusk that evening, Mattie Poor was surprised to see Lame Bear lying on top of his covers on the bed he shared with Sky. Usually when he returned from his bad times, he would build a fire to heat the rocks for the *osi*, their little domed steam hut, and then quietly disappear out back to remove his soiled clothing and wrap himself in his old blanket.

Returning to the *osi*, he would purify his body with the moist heat, and then, unless it was very cold, make his way down to the river to bathe before retrieving his other set of drawers and vest from his wooden peg on the cabin wall. Only then would he fall into bed.

Somehow, this time, Mattie Poor had missed him. She realized he must have come home earlier in the afternoon and cleaned himself up while she was away at her special canebrake by the river. She wondered, though, why he hadn't used the *osi*.

She sighed as she watched him sleep. Each time he left, she hoped it would be for the last time and that he would finally be able to stop drinking.

Realistically, however, she knew it was not to be. Still, she never gave up hope and also never stopped feeling deep disappointment each time it happened.

"Anyway, I'm glad he's home safe and sound," she thought as she turned to collect an assortment of tin cups, pewter spoons, and enamel plates from the pine shelves beside the mantel.

Three days ago, the morning Lame Bear had left, Mattie Poor remembered seeing him at daybreak before the twins were up. He was working around the place, like he did most days, dressing and salting meat in front of the smokehouse. Later she'd seen him stretching and tacking up beaver and red fox pelts onto the side of the barn. When he saw her come out of the cabin to fix the morning meal, he was the one who'd suggested that, after they had eaten, they should go to the North Slope to collect the white oak she needed every year for her double weave lightening baskets.

Even with the two of them, the work of felling and striping the young trees was backbreaking and the trip had taken the better part of the day. After they had hauled home the wood and stacked it in the barn, instead of sitting down for a well-earned rest like she had, Lame Bear had quietly taken his leave.

She had watched him limp off on his clubfeet, with a sack of beaver pelts slung over his shoulder. When he got past the barn he'd turned and started up the trace on his way, she was sure, to get moonshine at Moogan's still.

It saddened her to see him go but she made no effort to stop him. She knew he'd trade some of his skins to Old Man Moogan for the rotgut he craved and then, liquored up, continue on into the town of Ellijay, where he'd drink some more. If he had any skins left by then, she'd heard that he'd probably try to buy time with a lady of the night before making his way back home.

Since Sweetwater's death, he had gradually slipped back into his old ways. She realized, however, that like before, he had to be the one to work things out.

Each time he wandered off, she tried to attend to business at home as if nothing was wrong, moving from one chore to the next in her usual fashion. The children were already accustomed to their father's hunting and trapping trips and accepted these absences, too. But, although they never spoke of it, Mattie Poor knew that Hettie, at least, understood very well the difference.

Trying not to awaken him, Mattie Poor quietly finished loading the supper dishes into her apron, and carried them outside to where Sky and Hettie were waiting.

She set down the bulky utensils on the rocks next to the fireplace and began to sort them out.

"Lame Bear's asleep in there," she said to Hettie, nodding towards the cabin. "I didn't see him come in, did you?

"Likely, he won't be ready for any food until tomorrow, at the earliest," she said, "but, for sure, he'll be plenty thirsty when he wakes up."

Hettie looked surprised as she studied her grandmother's face and waited for more information. Getting none, she stood up and reached over for the family's tin cups, lining them up one by one on the stone ledge. Without a word, she ladled out the cool spring water from the bucket.

Picking up Lame Bear's dented old cup, she turned toward the cabin. Sky immediately jumped up to go after her, but Mattie Poor, anticipating his movements, caught his arm and then pointed twice at the ground. He whimpered softly, and followed Hettie with his eyes, but when he got no reprieve from his grandmother, settled back down.

He was almost immediately distracted, anyway, by the enticing aroma of the peach cornmeal stuffing coming from the blackened possum that Mattie Poor was slicing. He stood up again, this time tensing his back and trembling ever so slightly, as he watched her saw back and forth through the crunchy skin and down between the back bones into the moist, white meat.

She placed three thick glistening chunks onto his dappled blue enamel plate and then spooned lumpy mounds of the fragrant stuffing beside the meat. Finally she angled the bowl of his pewter spoon into the stuffing, leaving the handle sticking up like a shiny flag, before handing him the plate.

He waited politely until she dismissed him with an outward wave of her arm. Then, smacking his lips in anticipation of the first mouthful, he used both hands to carefully carry the heavy plate of steaming food over to his usual eating-place just a short distance from the fire.

Hettie returned from the cabin. She took Sky his cup of water and then watched while Mattie Poor dished up her portion of the roast. Accepting her plate, she too retreated to her special rock just beyond Sky's.

She set her cup down on the ground, and then, settling back comfortably against the trunk of the gnarled and scarred old oak that shaded their cabin, she slowly, almost dreamily, began to eat while she pondered the strange and exciting events of the day.

She'd seen Sergeant Stone a number of times before, mostly around nearby Ellijay and the fort in New Echota, but she remembered him best from one evening several months ago when he'd come knocking politely at their door.

"Good evening, Sir," Benjamin Stone had said to Lame Bear when he opened the door.

"It's been reported that this household is still in possession of a hunting rifle, and under the law, Cherokees are not permitted to own firearms.

"I'm going to have to confiscate it, Sir," he'd said almost apologetically. "I'm under orders. Would you please bring it to me?"

He waited just inside the doorway while Lame Bear, without a word, crossed over to the fireplace, reached up and unhooked the rifle from its place over the mantle, and then carried it back to him.

Hettie, sitting at the plank table helping her grandmother card wool, had stared curiously at this tall young man with the quiet demeanor. When their eyes met, he'd surprised her with a wave of his hand and a shy smile. Until then, she hadn't realized he'd even noticed her across the darkened room. She remembered she'd gotten up then and joined her father at the door to get a better look at this interesting young man as he politely accepted Lame Bear's rifle.

She put down her spoon and laid her plate absently on the ground beside her. Smiling to herself, she leaned back again and closed her eyes.

"He may be a white boy and maybe he is like all the rest of them, the way Mattie Poor says, but he sure doesn't act like it to me, and I wouldn't mind seeing him again.

"No, Sir, I wouldn't. Not at all. Even if he isn't one of us."

CHAPTER 6

THE ROUNDUP BEGINS

Lame Bear's farm
Saturday, May 26, 1838

The next morning, just after sunrise, Hettie came out of the cabin struggling to button the top of her pink calico dress. Mattie Poor, leaning over the fire-ring, turned and gave her a quizzical look.

"It's getting too small. See? It hardly wants buttoning," Hettie explained.

Then she shrugged. "May as well wear it out now."

Truthfully, she did not know herself why she'd put on her second best dress instead of her old linsey-woolsey work smock. She just knew that she felt different today, more feminine and grownup. She was relieved, though, when Mattie Poor went back to fixing the fire without fussing at her.

In fact, Mattie Poor was surprised but not unhappy that Hettie was dressed so nicely. Today would be a good time to send her over to Halfmoon's place to see when the two elderly sisters could come over for a day of soap making.

"I saw yesterday the grease crock's about full and there's plenty of that old brown lye water in the bottom of the ash barrel too," Mattie Poor said to Hettie, "and, don't you know, it's already our turn to have the soap making here again."

She raked down to the live coals she'd carefully saved last night by burying them under a blanket of ashes. As she uncovered the smoldering deep red embers, she threw in handfuls of leaves and twigs. When they caught, she topped it all off with the half-burned log she'd set to the side after yesterday's fire.

"So this morning, take Sky and go to Halfmoon and Gertrude's place and tell them tomorrow or the next day, either one, will be good for us," she said, fanning the fire with her apron.

"Now go get Sky out of bed while I make the corncakes. You hear me?"

Even with the help of the sisters, Mattie Poor knew that making soap would take the better part of a day. To start, she'd hang her biggest kettle on the iron crane over the outdoor fireplace so that the animal fat from the crock would already be tried into tallow before Halfmoon and Gertrude arrived.

Then, as soon as she spotted them coming down the trace, she'd add the first bucket of lye water to the grease and the really hard work would begin. For several hours, the three of them would take turns cooking and stirring the mixture, adding more lye water as it boiled off until the mixture got very thick.

Only then, when the paddle left a pathway through the contents of the kettle, would they add some salt as a fixative, and maybe a handful of sweet pine needles for scent, and finally pour it out to harden in their collection of old wooden flats.

Even so, Mattie Poor reasoned, the three of them enjoyed each other's company and the time would pass quickly. If they got an early start, by mid-afternoon the soap would be cool enough to cut into soft bars, and the frail sisters, pulling their rickety old cart behind them, would still be able to make it home before sundown.

And so it was that Hettie and Sky, with his third corncake of the morning warm and crumbly in his hand, set off along the trail for Halfmoon's place. It was a long way but with the weather nice like it was today, they would both enjoy the trip. When they were younger, Hettie used to tie a long cord from her waist to his to keep him from straying but he was good now about staying close.

The azaleas in the woods along the way were almost finished blooming and the wind was carpeting the earth with their pink and white petals. Cobwebs of the morning dew hung like a lace canopy over the forest floor. After the heavy smoky atmosphere around the cabin, the mountain air, thick with the earthy smell of dark green ferns and rotting leaves, seemed mysterious and alluring to Hettie.

She began to feel excited about the prospect of a day without the same old chores. It was nice to get away and she didn't mind visiting with Halfmoon and Gertrude. One of them, probably Gertrude, would prepare a noon meal for them and then it would be time to head back home. The last time when they'd left, Gertrude had given them each a still warm sack of baked and salted pecan halves for the trip home. She licked her lips at the memory of the salt on her tongue and the crunchiness of the nuts between her teeth.

Hettie decided to stay on the main trail this morning and not try to take the overgrown shortcut because she did not want to tear her special dress. It was the one she'd worn during the five days last summer when she and Sky were allowed to stay with the missionary family way over in New Echota to learn Sequoyah's Cherokee writing.

Folks said that, in the beginning, everybody thought Sequoyah, who limped worse than Lame Bear, was just an old drunk. He was so crazy, she'd heard, that even his own wife had turned him out, and he ended up living in a tumbled-down shack until that burned to the ground.

But nothing was going to stop him, they said, and about fifteen years back, he'd finally figured out a way to turn all the Cherokee sounds into squiggly little charcoal lines on pieces of birch bark. Now, thanks to him, Cherokees had talking leaves just like the white people.

During the all-day reading and writing lessons which were taught by the missionary's wife, the adults and the older children recited and practiced their symbols while the younger boys and girls sat on the hard packed dirt floor of the Council House listening or playing quietly nearby.

Each morning, after the first day when she realized the work was going to be too hard for Sky, Hettie settled him at the back of the section where the Wild Potato Clan normally sat. He was usually a good-natured boy and liked being with the other children but sometimes he got upset if they touched his special bag of marbles. Hettie knew he'd be better off by himself.

Lame Bear had given him the marbles along with a deerskin pouch in which to keep them. They originally belonged to Tahchee, the young son from Lame Bear's first family who, along with his mother and sister, had died many years ago from smallpox. There were twelve marbles in all, real agates, not homemade balls of clay like most of the other New Echota youngsters had.

Sky didn't care that he was off by himself. In fact, most days, he settled right down to begin his favorite game. First, he positioned his marbles in a circle around his most special one, a green and yellow cat's eye. Then, tucking his thumbnail behind the knuckle of his forefinger, he'd aim and flick the marbles, one by one, trying to hit the cat's eye in the center. When he grew tired, he would curl up on the dirt floor for a nap, and then start the process all over again until it was time for Hettie to come for him.

Earlier, when the classes were announced, Hettie couldn't hide her disappointment when she found out that her father and grandmother were not coming.

"Child, I can't be wasting my time like that," Mattie Poor said. "There's too much to be done around here."

Hettie felt like saying, "Then how come you can find time year after year for those boring Council meetings you drag us to? And why does Lame Bear have to tend his traps again so soon, anyhow? He just got back."

But she held her tongue out of respect for this hard working old woman who'd raised her. Still, even without Mattie Poor and Lame Bear, the lessons had turned out to be fun and not nearly as hard as she'd expected. Hettie felt proud and very grown up to be the only reader in her family.

On the first day of the lessons, she remembered, this same Sergeant Stone who'd been in the orchard yesterday had appeared at the doorway of the Council House to have a word with Mrs. Miller, the missionary's wife. After looking around to see who was inside, his gaze had settled on her.

"Hello," he called, "How are you this morning?"

She was surprised and secretly pleased that it was she, and not the Wolf Clan girl, who had caught his attention. From then on, each morning when she got to the Council House, she had hoped he'd come again, but he never did.

The state of Georgia had managed to shut down *The Cherokee Phoenix* Printing Office several years before Hettie attended Mrs. Miller's classes, but old copies of the bilingual newspaper still circulated. Now, each time her family could get hold of an issue, Hettie would sit down by the fireplace in their best chair, the rocker Mattie Poor had caned herself. Using her pointing finger to keep the place, she would carefully enunciate each syllable from the Cherokee columns. Even Sky, who had shown no interest during the classes, sat motionless, hypnotized by her rhythmic rocking and the movements of her lips, until she had finished every word.

It was from the *Phoenix,* as well as from Council meetings and conversations with their neighbors, that the family learned more about the efforts of the Cherokee leaders, especially Council Chief John Ross, to hold onto their land and to fight for their rights through legal appeals to the United States courts. Chief Ross and the other leaders had even appealed directly to President Andrew Jackson, as well as to the United States Congress in Washington.

But it was also from neighbors that the family learned of the Federal Government's latest efforts that allowed the State of Georgia to raffle off their land to whites and to try to force all of the Cherokees to relocate to reservations far away in the west, beyond the Arkansas River.

Everyone was worried and sick at heart. Hettie recalled that Lame Bear had declared,

"We must not give up any more land. Too much has already been lost. What the whites call Georgia, Tennessee, Kentucky, Alabama, most of the Carolinas and even parts of Virginia, these are really our lands, taken from us in false treaties," he'd said.

"We'll give up no more of our land to them. And we'll never leave our mountains," he'd sworn. "Never."

Hettie remembered that Mattie Poor, on the other hand, had only shrugged.

"Well," she'd said. "You know, we've only ourselves to blame for trusting those lying whites and for always trying to be like them!

"Let me tell you one thing," she'd scolded. "Folks need to go back to the old ways, and start respecting our clans and villages like before. So there."

But today was a perfect day for a trip to Halfmoon and Gertrude's place and Hettie brushed aside these concerns. Suddenly she caught sight of Fort Mountain off to the northwest. Usually shrouded in thick clouds, today it was stark and clear and looked close enough to touch.

Look, Sky," she signed after catching hold of his arm to get his attention. She pointed.

"There's Fort Mountain, our family's special mountain."

Making the signs for mother and for long ago, she pretended to pick berries as she said,

"Mattie Poor says that years ago, when Sweetwater was a little girl, they used to go berrying up there, not just for the mulberries that are supposed to be the best in the whole Cherokee Nation, but also for the blackberries and gooseberries that grow there too.

"Their farm was way over yonder, right about in there somewhere, beside their special river—see that little thing over there?" She made the sign for river and then wiggled her finger as she pointed.

They continued to walk in a comfortable but purposeful way, and before long, the sickening odor of fermenting mash from Moogan's still began to fill their nostrils. Sky wanted to turn onto the well-worn path towards the tumbledown shacks to see what smelled so bad, but Hettie anticipated his interest and was ready to gently nudge him forward. The fact that he couldn't hear the faint sounds of voices and laughter coming from behind the stand of sugar maples made it easier to distract him.

The path widened and became uneven from the heavy wear of the wagon traffic between Ellijay and the still. Hettie and Sky had to watch where they stepped to avoid the deepest ruts and the worst mud puddles. But they both knew that once they got to the top of the next hill they would be able to look across the valley and make out Halfmoon's cabin.

It was a tall chink cabin with a stone chimney, the only two-story building this side of Ellijay. Once, long ago, the upper level had been a sleeping loft for Halfmoon's children. During the year of the smallpox, however, the *Raven Mocker of Death*, after sneaking into Lame Bear's place and snuffing out the lives of his family, had swooped down on Halfmoon's and taken all three of her children, as well as her husband, Kookowee the *Shaman*.

It was then that her sister Gertrude had come to live with her to keep her company. Now they used the loft only for storage.

Sky ran ahead to be the first at the lookout point. But when he got there, something alarmed him. He began to grunt and wave frantically for Hettie to catch up.

Below, off in the distance, she could make out a small contingent of uniformed soldiers milling around Halfmoon's cabin. Farther away, a horse and wagon approached. Hettie could see a man and woman on the seat of the buckboard, which was heavily laden with furniture. There were two children perched in the back as well.

As Sky and Hettie watched in disbelief, they spotted the far-away figures of Gertrude and Halfmoon who were outside the door of their cabin, struggling with one of the soldiers. She recognized the soldier. It was Venable Guinnett, the soldier who'd been with Benjamin Stone in the apple orchard just yesterday. Both sisters were trying to get into the house but Venable was blocking their way. Gertrude was beating on his chest with her fists. Roughly, he pushed her away. She stumbled and fell. When Halfmoon tried to help her, he shoved her too.

Hettie was stunned. Her heart was pounding. Then she spotted a familiar figure standing off to one side with a rifle in his hand. It was Benjamin Stone. A surge of lightheadedness engulfed her and she felt warm little ripples inside her chest.

"Look Sky," she cried out as if he could hear her. "Benjamin's down there. Don't worry. He won't let anybody hurt them. You'll see. It'll be alright."

But it was not all right. As they watched helplessly Venable Guinnett took the butt of his rifle and waved it at the sisters. He began to poke and prod them from behind, pushing them along until they reached a small group of people Hettie hadn't noticed before who were crowded together under a tulip poplar tree beside the trail.

Hettie gasped as the gravity of the situation hit her. Sky sensed the danger too. Together they whirled around to take cover in the thick underbrush. Hettie's billowing skirt snagged on a branch, and held her prisoner for just an instant. Sky began to whimper and reach for her. She put her finger to her lips to calm him and a moment later was able to crouch down beside him.

Peering through the bushes, she saw Benjamin Stone walk over to join Venable Guinnett in ordering Halfmoon and Gertrude to move towards a small group of Cherokees standing under a tulip poplar tree. Hettie recognized the Pritchards, Halfmoon's next-door neighbors, who were huddled there with their arms around their two frightened little boys.

Struggling to stay calm, Hettie tried to think clearly about what to do. One way or another, she knew this meant her people were going to be forced to leave their Nation, and, what's more, Benjamin Stone was right in the thick of it.

She and Sky watched helplessly as Benjamin Stone positioned the Pritchards and the two sisters into a pitiful little marching formation. With Stone leading the way, and another soldier bringing up the rear, the party started off in the direction of New Echota and Fort Wool. As the procession turned out of the yard onto the trace, however, they had to step aside for the horse pulling the wagonload of household goods.

Hettie shuddered and withdrew further into the underbrush as she recognized the couple sitting up on the front seat. It was the Campbells, the family who had laid claim to Lame Bear's land through the Georgia state lottery. Slowly but surely, they were heading this way.

Meanwhile, Venable Guinnett waited until Benjamin Stone's prisoners were on their way towards New Echota before leading the rest of his comrades on towards Moogan's still. He knew there was always a chance that the removal might miss a few Indians. In fact, just a few moments ago, they'd heard noises and glimpsed a flash of pink calico up in the hills in front of them.

But so far he'd rounded up all the folks on his list and he knew that when the last of them was interned back at the Fort Wool Stockade, his lieutenant would be pleased. As a new recruit, he'd been surprised to be chosen for the removal. But he still had two more places to go before he could call it a day.

He'd made it a point to save Lame Bear's cabin for last, so he could be the one to bring in that buxom little gal himself, the one with the moon face and the big behind.

Ebb Tide

He carried Sweetwater down the worn path to the place in the stream where she and Mattie liked to do the washing.

CHAPTER 7

SOUNDING THE ALARM

Lame Bear's farm, the same day
Saturday, May 26, 1838

Sky was whooping and jabbering as he thrashed after Hettie through the underbrush along the shortcut. He didn't understand exactly why Halfmoon and Gertrude were in trouble with the soldiers, but he knew for sure that what they'd just seen was very serious and it made him afraid.

Now Hettie was going so fast she was almost running and he could hardly keep up. His ankle was hurting where he'd turned it and he was worried Hettie was going to leave him behind. To make matters worse, branches were ricocheting back and slapping at him even though he was doing his best to fend them off with his elbows.

For once, Hettie was glad he was making all that noise.

"At least I don't have to keep turning around to keep track of you," she thought as she pushed on.

The hem of her pink calico dress was being torn to pieces and she kept tripping on it, ripping it even more. Sharp twigs and brambles were scratching and jabbing at her unmercifully, and her arms and legs prickled and burned. It just made her more determined. She knew all would be lost if they didn't make it home ahead of the Campbells and the soldiers.

She was sure Mattie Poor would be there, waiting for them as usual, and she'd know what to do. Like always. But Hettie wondered what they'd do if Lame Bear were off somewhere. How could they warn him? But she didn't really think he'd be away checking traps. Most likely he'd still be feeling peaked today, probably not ready yet for much of anything.

Now Sky was beginning to cry, but each time she slowed down to let him catch up and to comfort him, she was haunted by the image of the Campbells relentlessly pressing forward in their buckboard, eager to take away their home.

She could just picture them huddled like vultures by the cabin door, waiting for the soldiers to catch up and let them in.

"Just like that," she thought, "they can steal everything we've worked for and Georgia won't do a thing to stop them. In fact, Mattie Poor says the idea for a land lottery came from the state in the first place.

"Those whites are evil," she seethed, "all of them. And Venable Guinnett and Benjamin Stone, they're just as bad as the rest."

Taking Sky by the hand and leading the way along the shortcut, she slowed her pace and tried to remember to hold back the branches for him. But each time she had to stop, she also frantically signed, "Hurry, hurry, hurry," before forging ahead again. In this fashion, they reached the clearing above the farm just as the sun was reaching its highest point of the day.

"Help! Mattie Poor, Lame Bear, where are you? Help!" Hettie screamed as she let go of Sky's hand and ran down the hill towards the barn. "We need help! Oh please! Somebody! Help!

"Where are you? Won't somebody help us? Quick! Help! Mattie Poor, Lame Bear, anybody," she shouted, "Help! Help!"

Pitchfork in hand, Lame Bear appeared in the doorway of the barn.

"What is it? What's the matter?" Alarmed, he hurried to meet them.

"The soldiers, they're coming! Just now, we saw the whole thing, Halfmoon and Gertrude getting arrested and all. Hurry! Please, please," she begged, grabbing his arm.

"Oh Mattie Poor," she cried as she spotted her grandmother coming out of the cabin. "You've got to do something right away. There's no time! They're coming for us!"

She struggled for breath as her chest heaved in and out. Her voice quavered and broke frequently as she blurted out the rest of the story. By the time she finished speaking, she was trembling all over. She covered her face with her hands and began to sob.

Sky was standing off to one side, trying to catch his breath, as he watched the drama unfold around him. When he saw his sister crying, he couldn't bear it. Putting his head back in anguish, he opened his mouth and began to keen, at first softly and then louder and louder until the valley was full of his eerie wailing.

Lame Bear placed his hand gently on his son's shoulder to quiet him but at the same time turned to Mattie Poor.

"We've got to decide right quick what to do, Mattie. The soldiers are likely to be here as soon as they finish up at Moogan's, probably within the hour.

"Are we going to hide out in that old hunting cave near the end of my trapping line like we said?" he asked her. "What do you say, Mattie? What do you want to do?"

Then he spoke to Hettie.

"Remember, Hester, that time you were helping me set out the traps and the snow came so sudden and we took cover in that cave by Turtle Rock and the waterfall? Remember that place? It won't be easy, especially when winter sets in, but we should be safe there, at least for now."

Again he faced the old woman, "What say you, Mattie?"

"I stand with you as always, Lame Bear," Mattie Poor answered quietly.

Lame Bear said, "Then so be it, Beloved Woman.

"We can hide some of our household things in the bushes up on the hill behind the graveyard. That way when we leave for the cave, we'll only have to carry food and such. And, Hester, you and I can come back later for our things. Go, now, with your grandmother and gather up what you can from the cabin. Quickly!"

He signed to Sky as he said, "Come on, Son, let's go to the barn and put our best tools in the wheelbarrow to hide them up there, too.

"We won't be long, Mattie," he called after them, "and then we'll be over to help you. Come on, Sky, let's go. Quickly."

He strode purposefully into the barn. Sky, reassured by his father's calmness, trotted docilely after him.

When they reached the cabin, Mattie Poor and Hettie set right to work. Mattie Poor's first act was to fill her special leather medicine pouch and tie it around her middle. There was no conversation at all between them about what to take and what to leave behind. They quickly placed utensils and other possessions onto the two blankets they'd spread out on the cabin floor.

Finally, sensing that time was running out, they stopped and together reached down to gather up one of the blankets by its corners. One of the smaller dented old pots clattered out onto the dirt floor.

"It's taking too long," Hettie cried. "We'll never make it."

But just then Lame Bear, with Sky right behind him, entered the cabin. The four of them managed to gather up the piles of household belongings and, by half dragging and half carrying them, haul them up to the graveyard on top of the hill. They hid their loads next to the wheelbarrow in the thick bushes just beyond the four small stones that marked the graves of Sweetwater and the three members of Lame Bear's first family.

Hurrying back down to the cabin, they threw burlap bags of dried beans and corn, along with slabs of cured meat from the smokehouse onto the last of their blankets and quilts.

"What about the mule?" Hettie asked, suddenly remembering that gentle animal in the barn.

"They'd spot his tracks and follow us, Hester, and besides, how would we feed him up there in the mountains? We'll have to leave him here." Lame Bear said.

"It'll be hard enough as it is with all the noise Sky makes. Now, let's get moving."

Awkwardly, they maneuvered their unwieldy bundles out the door. Hettie, the last to leave, turned back to take one final look around. As she squeezed herself and her load through the doorway, a tiny scrap of her pink calico dress caught on a splinter of the threshold.

Chapter 8

The Escape

The Great Smoky Mountains
Later the same day
Saturday, May 26, 1838

Single file, the little family began its journey into hiding. Heading upstream towards the mountains, they stayed close to the banks of the river, scaling rocks and boulders when they couldn't go around them, pushing their way through thick grasses and underbrush, and gradually climbing higher and higher beyond the foothills and into their mountain sanctuary shrouded in swirls of lavender mist.

They were bent almost double under the heavy packs on their backs. Lame Bear was positioned at the front. He and Mattie Poor kept Sky wedged between them so that Hettie, taking up the rear, was free to cover their tracks.

Sometimes it was just a question of scuffing away the evidence of their passage with the toe of her moccasin or perhaps smoothing out the tall grass with her knee, but at other times she had to stop and put down her load in order to erase deep footprints in the soft sand or replace dry leaves that had been kicked aside. It was tedious and tiring work and the others had to keep stopping to wait for her but no one doubted its importance.

It was growing dark and their destination in the mountains was still several hours away. Sky was becoming more and more irritable and Lame Bear knew they had started too late in the day to go all the way tonight. It was just too far.

As he led the way, Lame Bear started looking for a place where they could rest for the night. Up ahead he eventually spotted a fallen fir tree, its roots upended into a giant mushroom shaped ball of dirt. In the past, he'd spent many nights in such places.

Turning to Mattie Poor, he said, "We can't go much further today." He pointed to the tree. "Think that hollow under those roots up there will do for one night?"

"It looks alright to me," she said, hitching up her load, "a good enough place to rest, away from the wind and all. And we should be far enough along by now for a small cooking fire. It'd be hard for them to spot our smoke in all this mist anyhow."

After stowing their gear in the deepest part of the little shelter formed by the tree roots, they made their way carefully through the sharp marsh grass guarding the riverbank. Hettie walked off to the side by herself and got behind a tree. She gathered up the torn skirts of her once beautiful dress, pulled down her drawers, and squatted down so that she could relieve herself. Then she followed the others over to the water's edge.

Kneeling on a rock alongside the bank of the stream, she cupped her hands and dipped them into the clear water. Then she lowered her face into her palms, puckered her lips, and guzzled the water, again and again, until her thirst was slaked.

After climbing back up the bank, Hettie and Sky set about collecting underbrush and pieces of seasoned wood. They quickly found enough for the fire, delivered it to the tree hollow, and then flopped down to rest while Lame Bear and Mattie Poor prepared the camp. With his fingers, Sky brushed out a smooth circle in the sand beside him and pulled out his deerskin pouch of marbles.

Lame Bear used pieces of flint from the little tinderbox he always kept in his pocket to produce a spray of sparks, which eventually ignited his stack of dry leaves. He then blew gently on the flickering pile, nursing it along until it produced a steady flame to which he gradually added twigs, branches, and rotten bits of Hettie and Sky's wood until he was satisfied that the fire was suitable for cooking and, later on, for discouraging foraging animals.

Hettie watched as Mattie Poor rearranged the provisions to make more room for sleeping later on, and then methodically picked out two long straight sticks from the kindling pile. By sharpening the ends with her caning knife, she turned them into roasting skewers. Next she sliced off chunks of the smoked ham she had carried on her back all day, threaded them onto the sticks, and handed them to the twins to cook over the fire.

Then she rummaged in her apron pocket and found the supply of corncakes she'd baked that morning and thought to bring along. They were flattened and soggy but Hettie and Sky couldn't keep their eyes off them.

It had been a long time since they'd been this hungry, but after doling out the meat and corncakes, Mattie Poor rewrapped everything and pushed the sacks to the back of the hollow. There would be no second helpings tonight. Hettie and Sky cooked their meat rations over the fire and savored the precious crumbs from the corncakes.

After the meal, Lame Bear leaned back against a burlap sack of corn, with a fire-tending stick resting lightly in his hand, and watched as the Great Spirit began to spread out the blanket of stars. When it got dark enough, he pointed his stick at the first bright star. Then he searched for the Dipper Gourd, and pointed that out too.

"See how the Great Spirit is lowering the bowl of his dipper and offering us water?" he said. "And, look, way up high, there's the Guide Star. You can always find it by sighting upward from those last two stars of the Dipper Gourd. Right up there, see? If ever you lose your way, all you need do is wait for the night, because, unless it's raining or very cloudy, the Guide Star will always try to show you the way. It stays in its place, night after night to help us, and does not move around like the other stars."

Sky tried to figure out what his father was pointing to as he played with his marbles by the firelight, but he soon grew sleepy and lost interest. He dropped his marbles one by one into his deerskin pouch, pulled the drawstring tight, and curled up under the blanket that he would share with Lame Bear.

Hettie, however, hugging her knees and looking up at the Sky Dome, wanted Lame Bear to continue even though she'd heard it all many times before.

"Tell us how the earth began, Lame Bear. Tell us about the Water Beetle."

Lame Bear cleared his throat and inserted the deep characteristic grunt that all Cherokee elders used among their words when they were teaching.

"This is what the old men told me, *guh*, when I was a boy.

"A long time ago, the world below had only water and all the animals and people lived up above. But finally the world up there got too crowded, so Water Beetle decided he'd try to help.

"One day he came down and dove deep into the water. When he finally got to the bottom, he discovered it was covered with mud. He took in a big mouthful.

"When he rose to the surface again, he spat out the mud. It gradually spread over the top of the water until it shaped itself into a trembling island. The people and the animals were watching Water Beetle from above and when the mud had dried and they saw what he had done for them, they thanked him and decided to call it earth. Then they moved down here where they've been ever since.

"And that is what the old men told me when I was a boy," he said, finishing with a grunt.

"Where in the Sky does the Great Spirit live, Lame Bear? How come we can't see him?" Hettie asked.

"The Great Spirit lives all the way over at the far end of that long white road up there. See how it goes from one side of the Sky Vault to the other? Look how long it is!" he said as he made a sweeping motion with his stick.

"His home is so far away, no one's ever seen him."

Hettie asked, "Well, if he's such a good Spirit, like you and Mattie Poor always say, how come he let our mother die? Huh? Answer me that." She needed to hear this part again too.

Lame Bear was quiet for a moment before he spoke.

"The Great Spirit needed Sweetwater with him in the Sky and so he sent his messenger, the Mighty Hunter, to bring her back to him. We can't see the Hunter tonight, but you remember what he looks like, don't you, with his belt of jewels and his long sword?

"The Mighty Hunter came down and took your mother back to live on the Sky Rock," Lame Bear continued, "and, sometimes, you can almost see her in the ring of stars where she lives with the other Cherokee women. They are called the Seven Sisters because they are all members of the Wild Potato Clan like you and Mattie."

Mattie Poor, who had been listening while she finished her meal, spoke up as she began to tell her part of the story,

"Well, let me tell you one thing. When you and Sky entered this world beside New Town Road in New Echota, you came from a special place on the Sky Rock too, very near to your mother's circle of stars."

Lame Bear pointed over to the west, just above the horizon.

"See, over there, the Star Twins standing tall, side by side? Over there?" he said. "See them? Look! They're just now climbing out of the mountains, as they do most nights, to join their father, the Great Spirit."

Mattie Poor said,

"See how they have their arms wrapped around each other? That's how you and Sky were when you were born.

"Your birth was very special. You, Hester, were in such a hurry to get down out of the sky that you were already reaching out with your little hands towards the earth, trying to touch it with your fingertips.

"Sky, on the other hand, well, that's another matter," she said, smiling as she glanced over at his sleeping form. "He wanted to stay up there with the Great Spirit. All the while he was being pushed through to the earth, he kept stretching his little arms back up to the Sky Rock, begging the Great Spirit to take him back."

Lame Bear took over again.

"Every year, just after the Green Corn Ceremony, the Star Twins are high in the Sky, way up there, next to the Guide Star. You can see them most every night and, what's more, they stay there right on the top of the Sky Rock protecting us during the long winter nights too. They're all up there—your mother and her Cherokee Sisters, the Star Twins and even the Mighty Hunter too—all of them together."

Mattie Poor said, "Some Cherokees who don't know any better think twins are unlucky, but in our village we have always known that double births bring good fortune.

"Why, since you and Sky came, we've had many long gentle summer rains and corn and beans to spare almost every year. More squash too. And, today, escaping from the soldiers, that was another good omen."

Mattie Poor stopped abruptly.

"But for goodness sakes, Hester," she said irritably, "That's enough for one night. Lie down now and go to sleep."

Hettie and Sky

They sat, periodically turning the handle of the spit so that the meat would roast evenly, and waited for their grandmother to come home.

CHAPTER 9

THE STOCKADE

New Echota, Georgia
Late May, the same year (1838)

Benjamin Stone thought he was used to the way the military did things, but he'd never seen anything like this. The Cherokees, rounded up under General Winfield Scott's orders, were jammed like cattle into the Fort Wool Stockade at New Echota. Every now and then a few more stragglers were brought in. The guards just opened the gates and mindlessly shoved them in.

Even though it wasn't even June yet, the heat was already intense. Each morning when the sun came up, its merciless rays oozed like molten lava over the stockade grounds. The bewildered Cherokees sweltered as they huddled there, hour after hour, and day after day.

When the sun finally set, their suffering seemed to ease, but very soon the night air became damp and then cruelly cold. Many Cherokees were rounded up without any coats or blankets and others were not even given time to find their shoes. They awoke in the mornings chilled to the bone and barely able to walk to the latrines. Almost daily, one or two of the old people, especially those already weakened by the coughing sickness, lost hope altogether and seemed to choose not to awaken at all.

Soon many of the diseases that had long plagued the white man came and hovered like evil spirits over the camp. When no one was looking, they crept silently into unsuspecting, defenseless bodies.

Children stopped playing. Little ones, just beginning to crawl or walk, who used to need constant watching, grew dazed and listless and became easy to keep track of.

The flies darted back and forth between the open latrine ditches and the food wagons. The presence of so much human waste sent them into a feeding and stinging frenzy. Attracted by runny noses and sticky little eyelids, the flies, after satiating themselves on excretion and rotting food, burrowed their way into the already festering tear ducts of the smallest Cherokees to lay their eggs.

Ben used to like all his Georgia National Guard assignments: guard duty, surveying work, marching in parades, training new recruits, taking inventories, or searching for fugitives. But no more. He had no stomach for what was happening at Fort Wool.

Nowadays, when he had to be on duty, the terrible stench coming from the latrines at the opposite corners of the stockade grounds seeped into his uniform, his hair, and his skin. He swore he could smell it even when he slept. As he patrolled the grounds, he tried to breathe through his mouth, but eventually his throat became so parched he couldn't stand it.

Then someone told him about soaking the cuffs of his uniform blouse in horse liniment before his tour started and using that as a shield. He found it helped some, at least for the first few hours anyway.

At last, when he had earned a few days leave, he saddled his beloved Sonny and escaped to his parent's tobacco and cotton farm just beyond Dalton, Georgia. He needed the warm and accepting environment he always found there as well as the time away from the stockade to sort out the difficult new thoughts and feelings he was experiencing.

Ben's mother, always happy to see him, set right to work scrubbing his uniform for him while he sat in the tin bathtub just outside the three room log cabin with the wattle and daub chimney where he'd grown up. He washed his face and head first, working up a lather as he used his fingers to massage the homemade soap into his hair, submerging completely to rinse off, and then repeating the process. Next, he methodically began to scour the skin on the rest of his body as he tried to wash away the memory of the stockade smell.

After drying himself off with a tattered piece of flannel, he pulled on a pair of his outgrown overalls, which belonged to his younger brother Gabriel now. The legs were so short on him they looked almost like knickers, but the worn fabric felt soft and sensual against his bare skin, especially along the line of silky fur running down the center of his stomach. It tingled every time he took a step.

He was normally a quiet boy but his mother sensed right off that, this time, he had something more on his mind than just dirty clothes. There was no use questioning him. She knew he would get around to telling her in his own way and in his own good time.

While waiting for his father and Gabriel to return from the fields, Ben helped her wring out his wash. Then he carried the two-handled oval wicker basket along with the drawstring bag of clothespins over to the line behind their homestead.

One by one, he handed his mother the wooden pins that long ago had been his soldiers when he played army. She hung the clothes methodically, beginning with the heavy uniform pieces, followed by his linen vest, underdrawers and stockings, and ending with a row of his blue and white cotton bandannas.

Off in the distance, across the newly planted red clay fields, Ben caught sight of his father and brother making their way home. When they spotted him, Gabriel, five years younger, let out a whoop and broke into a dogtrot. As he waited, he was reminded of another time and another boy of about the same age whom not so long ago had also been happy to see him. He wondered what that boy would think of him now after what Ben and the others had been done to his people.

After his father and Gabriel washed off the day's grime at the springhead, the family gathered inside the simple cabin while his mother prepared supper. He and Gabriel set the plank table as they always did, and when the food was ready, helped move the heavy dishes from the hearth to the long centerboard of the table.

It was good to be home again. He felt better already as they joined hands.

"Bless, oh Lord, this food to our use and us to thy faithful service," his father intoned. "And thank Thee, dear Lord, for bringing us all together again. Amen."

"Amen," they replied.

They ate in silence. Only the raspy droning of the cicadas outside and the scraping of their metal forks on the plates broke the quiet. After supper when the dishes were washed, dried, and put away in the corner hutch, Ben pulled his chair around so that he could face the hearth. Then he gradually tipped back until he felt the edge of the table.

Clasping his fingers together at the nape of his neck, he stretched out his long legs, crossed his bony ankles, and propped his bare feet on the oiled black anvil beside the fireplace.

Finally he felt ready to begin the story he had come so far to tell.

CHAPTER 10

THE CAVE

The Great Smoky Mountains
Late May 1838

The cave was even worse than Hettie remembered. The floor was covered with animal droppings and puddles of stagnant water. The walls were streaked with dried bat dung.

"I don't remember it like this," she mumbled to Lame Bear. "How are we supposed to live here? It stinks worse than the Pritchard's hen house. I feel sick."

She looked around for a dry place to put down her bundle. Disgusted at what she saw, she went back outside the mouth of the cave to place her load on the stone ledge. Sky, on her heels as usual, did the same.

"Don't forget, Hester, it was winter when we were here before and very cold besides. You wouldn't notice the smell so much," Lame Bear said, amused at her discomfort.

Mattie Poor was already giving orders, handing each twin a long stick to sweep across the ceiling of the cave to get rid of the bats while she began using a flat piece of bark to clear away the standing water and animal feces.

The bats emitted high-pitched screams as they were herded outside. Sky shrieked with laughter at the sight of them and then, suddenly, clapped his hands over his ears. At first Hettie thought he was trying to protect himself as the frantic bats rushed past. But then she wasn't so sure.

"Look at Sky, Mattie Poor," she shouted. "Look what he's doing!"

Mattie Poor swung around, but too late. Sky was already running around again, chasing more bats.

"Get to work," she said crossly to Hettie, turning her back again.

That night they covered the entrance to the cave with a blanket to keep the bats from returning and the light of the fire from showing. Eventually the walls and the floor dried out, and, before long, everything smelled of smoke, just like at home.

Several weeks later when they had settled in, there was a full moon and Lame Bear decided the time was right to fetch the tools and household goods they had left behind. The next day, after their mid-day meal of boiled wild greens, he and Hettie set off.

The farm was a half-day away and they reached it, as planned, just before dusk. While waiting for darkness, they hid out in the underbrush behind the graveyard where they had a clear view of the log cabin below.

Hettie felt her eyes fill with tears as she looked down at their home. The Campbells had carried all of their furniture out into the yard and made a bonfire out of it. She could make out the blackened hulks of their beds, tables, chairs, even the butter churn and the *kanona* where they ground their corn. The remains of Sweetwater's walnut loom and spinning wheel, which Lame Bear had lovingly made over their first long winters together, were visible at the bottom of the pile.

And there, too, was the pitiful skeleton of Mattie Poor's precious rocker, lying on its side in the ashes. It was charred black and the cane seat was completely burned away. She was glad Mattie Poor didn't have to see that.

"What about Mrs. Miller's drawing of Sky and me?" she thought to herself as they waited for nightfall. "Is it still hanging on the wall? And how about my new blue gingham with the puffed petal sleeves? Has the Campbell girl helped herself to that too?"

"Look at all those holes they've dug down there by the stream," she whispered to Lame Bear. "What are they for, anyway?"

Lame Bear answered, "The whites, they think there's gold in our Nation. That's one of the reasons they want our land so bad. And it seems to me like that's all this Campbell family cares about. They're not taking care of anything. Look over there. Mattie's herb and vegetable garden's all gone to weeds already, and yonder too," he said, pointing to the bottomland, "why you can't even make out her flax and hemp patches anymore."

"What about the mule?" Hettie asked. "You think they're taking care of him, giving him water, feeding him, and mucking out his stall?"

"Hard to say," Lame Bear answered. "When it's dark I'll go down and check on him and all the other livestock, too. Wouldn't want to see any of them go without."

They waited until the moon came up and the Evening Star appeared. Soon thereafter, Lame Bear silently rose and crept down the hill along the edge of the clearing. At first, Hettie could make out his shadow as he made his way to the barn and the animal pens. Then nothing. She waited apprehensively.

All at once, she heard a welcoming whinny and knew Lame Bear must be at the barn. She loved that old mule. He was the same one who'd brought them all home that day sixteen years ago after she and Sky had been born by the side of the road in New Echota. He was a steady worker with a sweet nature and she hoped that the Campbells were taking good care of him.

Suddenly, out of the darkness, came a muffled but chilling squeal and then silence.

After a moment, the door to the cabin jerked open and backlighting from the fireplace inside gave Hettie a clear view of a huge, heavyset man in the doorway. Crouching slightly with the stock of a shotgun cradled in the crook of his arm, Obadiah Campbell loomed large and menacing as he peered out into the darkness.

"Who's there? Who are you?" he yelled, drawing himself up.

Hettie was afraid to breathe.

"Show yourself, you varmint or I'll blow your God damn head off!" he screamed. "Come on out of there now, nice and slow, you hear me?"

She saw him tilting his head as if to hear better and, at the same time, bringing his gun up into the firing position. As he slowly pivoted from side to side, it seemed to Hettie that he was trying to aim straight for her.

"You'd better git if you know what's good for you," he shouted, sighting down the barrel.

He turned to someone inside.

"I dunno," Hettie heard him say. "Most likely some of them God damned Indians sneaking around looking to steal from us. Probably puking drunk, too, like usual. Well, by God, I'll make 'em think twice if they try anything," he threatened. "This place is ours now, fair and square, and that kind of trash don't belong here no how. Never did."

Sick at heart, Hettie listened for any more sounds from the barn that might give away her father's position. She realized that if Mr. Campbell started in the direction of the barn, she'd have to try to distract him long enough for Lame Bear to get away. And then, she'd have to try to escape herself.

"But what if he catches me? And how would I ever find Lame Bear again?" she worried. "Maybe he'd think I'd started back to the cave by myself and leave without me."

She lay motionless. The fear building inside her body was unbearable and just when she felt she couldn't stand it anymore, Mr. Campbell lowered his shotgun, shrugged his shoulders, and turned to go back inside. Changing his mind, he turned back to face the darkness once again, hawked loudly and let fly with a glob of spittle before finally backing up once more and latching the door.

A short time later, Lame Bear reappeared, a heavy burlap bag of salt slung over his shoulder. His voice trembled with anger as he whispered,

"The mule wasn't even in the barn. The cow and the hogs are alright but they've got their own horse in the stall and our poor old mule was tied to a tree out back, no water or hay, his coat all matted, and the rope so short he couldn't even lower his head."

He added quietly, "His suffering's over now."

Earlier, while they'd waited for darkness, they had prepared for the trip back to the cave by packing wads of hay and weeds around the metal tools and cooking utensils in the wheelbarrow to keep them from clanking together. Everything was in readiness for their return trip.

With Lame Bear carrying a bulky load on his back, and Hettie pushing the piled-high wheelbarrow, they headed uphill again towards the mountains. Neither one spoke about what had just happened with Mr. Campbell.

Their return route was less direct because of the wheelbarrow. And even with the bright moonlight to guide them, they had trouble with their footing. Her ragged hem kept catching on the underbrush, and, all in all, it was slow going. As she had done before, she covered their tracks as they went, but now they didn't feel the same urgency as the last time, which was just as well because she couldn't really see in the moonlight.

In this manner, resting now and then, they reached the cave just at sunrise. After what she'd seen back home, the cave, with Sky standing beside the entrance waving, was an unexpectedly welcome sight.

CHAPTER 11

THE DREAM

The Stones' farm, Dalton, Georgia
Late May 1838

"Things are bad up at the stockade," Ben told his parents and Gabriel, as he stared at the flickering flames in the fireplace, "real bad. The Army's got all those Cherokees stacked in there tighter than logs in a woodpile.

"They're suffering something awful, the old people and babes especially. And there's not enough quicklime in the whole place to keep up with the stink from the latrines." He sighed deeply and closed his eyes.

"You know, some of those Indians were dirt poor to begin with, but just the same, none of them's used to living like that neither."

His eyes drifted back to the fire. "I don't know how those poor people stand it. They're a pitiful sight and it's just not right. I rounded up quite a few of them myself and I sure don't feel very good about it now.

"But now I need to talk to you about something different that's come up," he said, clearing his throat.

"I just don't know what to think anymore and I've only got a few days left to make up my mind. What it is, I've been asked to join a U.S. Army Infantry company under General Winfield Scott. It would be a promotion. I'd be a second lieutenant instead of a sergeant with more pay and a nice signing bonus besides, if I decide to go through with it."

"Why Ben that's wonderful," his mother said, patting his arm.

"They're looking for recruits to help relocate the Cherokees, first from Fort Wool over to the emigration depot at Rattlesnake Springs in Tennessee, and then all the way west," he said.

"So, if I do decide to make the switch, the worst part is, I'd most likely be assigned to one of those removal details taking those pitiful Cherokees to Indian Territory way out west past the Arkansas River."

"Hear tell, that's a mighty long, hard march over mountains and treacherous waters," his father said. "And folks around Dalton are saying it's more than 800 miles."

"That's a fact," Ben agreed, and then added, "and there's another problem too. After it's over, I might not be stationed back here again. I could just as easily end up somewhere else, and you know I'm not keen on leaving Georgia."

"Can't say I blame you," his father said.

"Still," Ben countered, "it'd be steady work and a lot more money besides. And pretty soon I'd have me enough saved for a small spread of my own.

As usual, Gabriel, who'd been listening intently, was full of questions.

"What'll happen to Sonny if you switch over?" he asked.

When Ben had reassured him that the Militia would let Sonny go with him as long as they got an Army horse in return, Gabriel wanted to know what the journey west would be like.

Ben described the preparations needed for such a large undertaking. To begin with, the Cherokees would have to be divided into parties of seven or eight hundred each. With parts of the trip being over water, enough barges and flatboats would have to be on hand along the way to hold all those people, their household goods, and their livestock. And there would have to be enough horses or mules and wagons to carry the old people and any others who couldn't walk, as well as to transport all those provisions for them.

And he also tried to explain, as best he could, what the Cherokees would be facing once they reached the Reservation.

"From what I understand," he said, "the land isn't just sitting there empty, waiting for them. Lots of other Indians are already there, Osages, Creeks, and the like. Somehow, they'll have to work it all out."

Finally, he turned to his parents, "So, I guess what I'm asking is, what would you do if you was me? Paw? Maw?"

His parents exchanged glances before his father answered,

"Well, Son, it looks to me like a grand opportunity for you, even though it comes at a terrible cost to the Cherokees. But give us a little time to think it over," his father said, looking over at his Ben's mother. "We can talk again tomorrow before you have to go back."

While the family had been gathered around the hearth, the daylight had faded, and shadows had oozed across the rafters and let the darkness creep in. Now silence settled over the farmhouse as the family members rose, one by one, to visit the outhouse or to start other preparations for turning in. As usual, he would be sharing a rope bed with Gabriel in one of the two small bedrooms.

Without taking off his overalls, he slipped under the patchwork quilt he had watched his grandmother piece together when he was a boy. He remembered how she used to save colorful remnants of leftover material and scraps of worn-out clothing, which she'd painstakingly stitch into nine-square blocks for the top of the quilt. Then using a much coarser needle filled with fat cotton twine, she'd knot the center of each block onto the plainer, muslin backing she'd already joined together from leftover flour sacks.

When he still lived at home, he used to fall asleep every night, his backside firmly butted up against his brother's, fingering the perfectly spaced soft cotton knots. Now, amid the familiar surroundings and memories of his childhood, he listened to his brother's quiet rhythmic breathing, and then drifted off himself. But towards morning, his sleep became troubled.

He dreamed he was on a three-day search mission, hunting for Cherokees hiding in the mountains above Ellijay. At first it seemed ordinary enough, but then something happened, and he found himself cut off from the other soldiers.

Just then he'd spotted Mattie Poor and her family crouching in the underbrush beside a stream. When they realized they'd been discovered, they jumped up and started running in all directions. Ben dismounted and began pursuing them on foot. Confused about whom to follow, he finally decided on Lame Bear.

Ben tackled him from behind, and they tumbled around on the ground with Ben ending up on top. But when he rolled the old man over, a strange thing happened. It wasn't Lame Bear at all that he had pinned beneath him. It was the girl, the one they called Hettie. The one he'd had his eye on for months.

She was struggling to get out from under him, looking up with startled, frightened eyes. She was panting from the exertion.

Instinctively, he lowered himself on top of her. Now he became aware of the rest of her warm body too. It seemed just right under him. He felt like he'd finally found something very precious.

With a puzzled look, she stopped struggling and their eyes met. He lowered his head and kissed her soft, full mouth. Hesitantly, at first, and then more firmly she began to respond to him just as he woke up.

"Is it possible that she wants me as much as I want her," he wondered as he blinked awake. He was afraid to believe it.

He thought about the shy little Cherokee girl named Hettie who no longer seemed so shy or so little as he got up and went outside to the springhead to wash up for the day. He knew with absolute certainty he had to find her again.

He knew one other thing, too. She wasn't so little anymore. In the past, he'd pictured her as a half-grown girl, but now, as he looked back, he realized that she had been a young woman for some time. And he knew that, somehow, he had to find her again, to spend time with her, and, hopefully, even to court her.

He thought back to the many times he'd seen her in New Echota and Ellijay and to the day he'd gone to their cabin to confiscate Lame Bear's rifle. The moment when their eyes had met across the room stood out in his mind. He remembered the ripple of excitement he'd felt at the time and he was fairly certain from the look in her eyes then that the feeling had been mutual. And when they'd met again in the apple orchard that day he and Venable had been doing the surveying, he had sensed that she was interested in him, too.

"How come I never noticed before how grown up she's gotten?" he wondered.

"I think I have a good chance to win her over for real," he thought, "and I'm going to try. But only at the right time and in the right way.

"Anyway, there's a heck of a lot that needs doing before I can approach her again," he vowed as he splashed water on his face. "I know that. But, you can bet, the next time I see her won't be in any old dream either," he promised himself.

"It'll be for real, that's for sure.

"First thing, though, I've got to find her somehow and ask her to forgive me for taking part in the roundup of her people, and then do what I can to try to make it up to her."

Chapter 12

Pot Scrubbers

The Great Smoky Mountains
Summer 1838

Hettie and her family spent the summer months hunting and gathering just like in the old days. The elders' thoughts were always on the winter ahead and nothing was left to chance.

During the evenings, Lame Bear made himself a blowgun to take the place of his confiscated rifle. Each night, after Mattie Poor and Hettie were done cooking, he patiently coaxed along the smoldering fire. After first straightening and tempering a suitable piece of yellow locust, he picked out small round coals and dropped them into the long shaft, tamping them down with a length of smaller-bore river cane until he had burned out a hollow just the right size for his darts.

Early on, he and Sky had built a sturdy latticework fish weir out of river cane interwoven with green willow branches, which they anchored underwater in a curve of the stream. The fish could swim in but not out. After finding themselves trapped, they would hover almost motionless, waiting for they knew not what.

Sometimes in the late afternoon Mattie Poor would send Sky by himself to fetch a few for their evening meal. And when there were enough to make it worthwhile, he and Lame Bear would haul a sackful back to the cave. After the fish were done flapping, Lame Bear would take out their innards and Sky would hang them in neat rows over a makeshift rack to cure by the fire.

To keep from being discovered, Lame Bear had moved his line of traps farther up the mountainside to the north side of the cave. Once or twice, early on, he and Hettie had spotted evidence of patrols, but not recently.

"We're safe," he told her, "at least for now."

And, so far, although they would have welcomed them, they had seen no signs of any other Cherokees.

"If there's any others," he said to Hettie one day as they checked and rebaited his traps, "they're most likely all the way over to Quallatown by now, over there near Soco Creek on the other side of Kuwahi.

"It's over there," he reminded her, "where Will Thomas, that white boy that Chief Yonaguska took as his own, managed to buy up all those plots of land and deed them over to our people.

"That Will Thomas," he said, "he sure knows how to turn the white men's laws right back on themselves. Much better than our Council ever did. Thanks to him, there's Cherokee folks over there, right now, farming their own places, and the Army, they can't touch them. Even now."

When the twins weren't helping Lame Bear, Mattie Poor had them spending the long summer days winnowing wild grains, and picking greens and berries. She showed them where to dig for wild potatoes and other edible roots, some Hettie had never even heard of before, like smilax and cowbane.

She taught them that even though the smell of the pokeweed bushes was sickening, their thick green and reddish stalks were safe to eat and especially good in the spring, but the berries, which made their mouths water just to look at them, were poisonous and had to be left alone. The roots too.

When it got closer to autumn, she taught them how to spread a blanket under nut trees like the chestnut, walnut, and pecan, and shake the branches to make them surrender their treasures. Sky would have them both laughing as he swung back and forth from the lower limbs, wildly exaggerating his movements, as the nuts cascaded onto their blanket.

Each afternoon when Hettie and Sky returned to the cave, no matter how tired they were, Mattie Poor put them to work again spreading their bounty on the ledges outside. And each morning, under her watchful eye, she had them working their way down the lines, turning and rotating yesterday's take towards the sun, and culling out produce that was ready to bring inside for safer, long-term storage or to throw away any that had spoiled.

In this way, the stacks of winter provisions in Mattie Poor's food repository at the back of the cave grew a little taller each day. But, still, she was never satisfied.

And always, no matter where they were or what else they were doing, she kept them on the lookout for pot scrubbers, those leathery green lumps of tripe lichen growing in the cracks of the surrounding rocks.

"Those are the ugliest things she's made us gather yet," Hettie signed to Sky when Mattie Poor wasn't looking.

"You just wait. You won't catch me eating those bitter old things." Pointing to them, she clutched her throat and made gagging motions for his benefit.

But Mattie Poor made such a fuss if they walked by even one of the pot scrubbers, that it became second nature for them to squat down and scratch them off with their fingernails and then slip them into their burlap shoulder sacks.

"You can do better than this," she'd mutter as she stooped over and fanned them out to dry, "lots better. You haven't got near enough, you hear?"

Gradually, however, over the summer, her pile of the shriveled and blackened pot scrubbers grew until it resembled a giant beehive. But, even so, she nagged for more.

"Folks'll tell you, there's many a lost or hunted Cherokee survived the winter on pot scrubbers alone," she'd scold. "And thankful to have them, too."

When they complained about all the work, Mattie Poor had an answer for that, too.

"Let me tell you one thing," she'd say. "When the cold sets in, there won't be any more food for us to gather, except maybe a few more nuts and pot scrubbers, so we'd best stock up while we can. Mark my words, after the snows come, it'll be a long time 'til spring.

"Now's the time to worry, not later when we're half starved. Come to think of it, we still don't have enough wood, either. First thing tomorrow, we'll take the wheelbarrow and get some more."

Sure enough, the next day, right after a morning meal of fried fish, huckleberries, and leftover cold sweet potatoes, she took them out scrounging for firewood with Sky pushing the wheelbarrow and she and Hettie filling it. Today she had the small tomahawk that Hettie and Lame Bear had brought back from the cabin and, as they went along, she hacked up the branches to fit into the wheelbarrow.

All day long, they made trip after exhausting trip, each time venturing in a slightly different direction. Later, at dusk, after they had hidden the last load nearby, Mattie Poor awkwardly dragged herself up over the rocks onto the ledge. With her arms full of kindling, she stood looking down on them. Hettie could see her chest heaving as the old woman struggled for breath.

Finally she called down to them, "After you fetch the water, you can both come in for the day.

"But before you come up for the last time, be sure to check that the wheelbarrow's covered and hid real good, you hear?" she ordered, as she ducked her head and disappeared into the cave.

Bringing in The Cane

Shyly, she hung her head as the pungent odor of his sweat, mixed with the sweet smell of his nearly new leather boots, filled the air around her.

Chapter 13

The Plan

Rattlesnake Springs, Tennessee
Fall 1838

Back in May when Ben had been ordered to take part in the roundup, his commanding officer had told him that the Cherokees would be detained in the Fort Wool Stockade in New Echota for just a short time. They were supposed to start for the west in a matter of days.

Instead, in June, the Cherokees at Fort Wool had been transferred to another stockade, an emigration depot, just over the Tennessee border in Rattlesnake Springs, where the conditions soon became just as dreadful as those in New Echota.

The days dragged on, and the misery in the camp became more and more unbearable to witness. Ben felt especially bad about Gertrude and Halfmoon because he knew he was responsible for bringing them in. He could hardly bear to face them each day when he came on duty.

One morning when it looked like it was going to be especially hot, he fixed a canvas awning for the two sisters along one side of the depot's jagged fence where they usually settled. But the next day when he went to check on them, a mother and her sick baby were there instead.

Halfmoon and Gertrude had just moved farther down the wall and were squatting on their haunches, wrapped in their shawls, with their baskets on the ground beside them. When he tried to talk to them they just stared off into the distance.

"They don't deserve this," he thought. "Why, they're just two old ladies not much different from my own Grandma. How on earth are they supposed to be able to survive a march of some 800 miles when they look half dead already," he asked himself and then just shook his head in disbelief.

Ben couldn't understand, either, why the preparations for the relocation were dragging on and on. First, they said the flatboats weren't ready, then they said there weren't enough wagons and the supplies hadn't arrived yet. The last he'd heard, they were saying they had to wait for General Winfield Scott's marching orders. It seemed to him, though, that they just came up with one excuse after another without any regard for the misery in the depot.

"Why don't they just get it over with, for heaven's sakes?" he asked himself. "From what I can see, the longer they put it off, the weaker these folks are going to get and the worse it'll be for them. If I had anything to say about it, they'd be long gone by now, you can believe that."

Even though Ben was now a second lieutenant in the United States Army, he hated the duty in this emigration depot just as much as when he'd been stationed at the stockade in Fort Wool and he'd do almost anything to get out of it. He found himself volunteering for special patrols and details as often as possible to avoid witnessing the endless suffering first hand. He was especially happy when the mission involved going over into the hills above Ellijay so that he could secretly look for signs of Hettie.

"Once I find the family's hiding place," he reasoned, "then I can begin to help them. But if they think they've been discovered, they'll just move on, so I have to be real careful. Otherwise I'll have to start all over again."

He was already familiar with much of the territory around Ellijay. Over the years, he and Gabriel had hunted and fished in many of these same foothills, and his surveying work with the Georgia Militia had covered even more.

On his own time, weekends especially, Ben also went out searching for Hettie. He'd often make the long ride over to Moogan's abandoned still, and, taking the smaller side trails, follow the stream beds which branched off from the main river he'd fished and swum in as a child. He sometimes found pockets of lush paradise he never knew existed but, unfortunately, no traces of Hettie. Even so, as he and Sonny ambled along, his thoughts were always of her.

One early morning, on such an excursion, he approached the clearing above Lame Bear's spread. The place looked deserted. When he got closer, he saw that the Campbells must have pulled out.

He looked into the barn and the outdoor pens, but except for some dried-out mule remains out back, he saw no signs of recent activity. He dismounted by the well to give Sonny a drink out of an old leaky wooden bucket he found there and was shocked at the sight of Lame Bear and Mattie Poor's burned out household belongings in the front yard. Shaking his head, he moved on to the log cabin.

The Campbell's had trashed that too. The putrid smell of the remains of their last meal left lying on the table turned his stomach, but, as he looked around, he noticed a very small scrap of pink cloth wedged under a splinter of wood on the threshold of the doorway. Curious, he stooped over to retrieve it. He was puzzled because he knew that he'd seen something very much like this not too long ago.

Suddenly, he remembered where he'd seen it before. The first day of the removal when they were all at Halfmoon's place, he'd heard a noise and had seen a quick flash of pink up in the hills above the valley. He realized now that it must have been Hettie and that what he held in his hand was a piece of her calico dress. He fingered it thoughtfully and lovingly.

"She must have been up there on that hill watching the whole time," he thought. "Why, I'll bet she saw everything, and rushed back here to warn her Paw and Mattie Poor. Well now, that explains how come they were the only family in these parts who got away from us that day."

He placed the tiny scrap of fabric between the leaves of his small leather document case and tied it shut. He carefully placed it deep in the inner pocket of his jacket, which he then removed and hung outside on a branch of an old oak tree near the cabin.

He spent the rest of the morning clearing out the Campbells' rubbish and garbage. He worked cheerfully, and as quickly as he could, sometimes almost running as he made his way back and forth to the trash pit behind the barn with load after load of rubbish. Even the sweat rolling through the thick curls of the sun-bleached hair on his chest down into the waistband of his trousers didn't bother him. He didn't care. Nothing could stop him now. He had a plan. A wonderful plan.

In his usual off-key fashion, he whistled an old campfire tune that was a favorite of his mother's as he carried the last load to the dump. Then, with a length of rope he found in the barn, he fashioned a new latchstring and secured the door.

Sonny, who'd been rooting around contentedly in Mattie Poor's overgrown garden, stood quietly while Ben tightened the girth on the saddle. He remounted and they pushed off into the early afternoon sun.

He was pleased with his two discoveries: the empty cabin and the scrap from Hettie's dress. Smiling to himself, he thought about the unexpected progress he'd made today.

Hours later, when he was within sight of the shadowy outlines of the depot at Rattlesnake Springs, he found comfort in the fact that he wouldn't have to stay here very long this time either. Before he had gone on his weekend liberty, he had already volunteered for the next search party being organized to hunt down a renegade Cherokee named Old Charley who was thought to be hiding with his family over on the other side of the mountains. That detail would be heading out in just a few days time.

Old Charley, along with his family, had managed to avoid the initial May roundup of the Cherokees. Later, they'd been found hiding out in the mountains, but when the Army tried to bring them in, there was a scuffle. Supposedly the soldiers had hassled Old Charley's wife for moving too slowly, and, somehow in the confusion, one of the soldiers had been shot and killed with his own rifle. Afterwards, Old Charley and his people had escaped and were now hiding in the hills again.

The word was out that if Tsali, the Cherokee name by which Old Charley was also known, could be captured, General Scott would agree to an informal amnesty for the hundreds of other Cherokees still thought to be in hiding in the mountains. Ben knew this would include Hettie and her family so he was happy to be part of the search party that in a few days would be out looking for the old man.

It was late when he and Sonny approached the stables that evening, and the private normally on duty was nowhere to be seen, so Ben unsaddled Sonny himself and walked him until he had cooled down. Then he put fresh water, hay, and straw bedding in his stall before leaving him for the night.

Hungry himself, he headed towards the officers' mess tent to see what was left over from the evening meal, and then as was his habit before turning in, he steeled himself against the smell and entered the emigration depot to check on Halfmoon and Gertrude.

He found them in their usual spot, sitting cross-legged with their backs resting against the pales. He hunkered down in front of them and offered them some hardtack. They each accepted a round, tucking it under their shawls.

"I think your old neighbors, Mattie Poor and her family, are safe," he said in a low voice, "and I've got a pretty good idea where they're hiding."

They both looked up at him, alarm showing on their usually stoic faces. He quickly reassured them.

"No, no, don't worry, I'm not about to give them away. Never. I know now that bringing in the two of you and all those others was a terrible mistake. I'm real sorry for doing it, and you have my word I'll never betray you or them again. Even if it means resigning my commission."

Speaking quietly, he went on, "I'll do my best to make it up to all of you, you'll see. Meanwhile, though, I aim to find their hiding place and help out in any way I can, so long as I don't have to disobey any direct orders."

He pulled out his case and removed the fragile bit of pink calico.

"Is this a piece of Hester's dress, do you know?" he asked holding it up. "Have you ever seen her wearing anything like this?

"I found it today, stuck in the doorway of their cabin, and you know what else? The Campbells, those folks that won their spread in the lottery, they've pulled out. Just like that. They about wrecked the place but at least they're gone.

"Say now, you recognize this or not?"

Neither of them spoke, but he wasn't surprised. He knew they didn't trust him. Why should they? He was just glad they accepted the extra food he brought them nearly every day. He realized he was lucky to have gotten that far with them even though he did wonder, sometimes, what they did with it.

But he had the answer he was looking for. He'd spotted the recognition on their faces when he'd held up the little pink scrap.

As he walked to his cubicle in the officers' quarters, he was already thinking ahead. First he needed to find out where the Campbells were living now. Next he'd collect his signing bonus and then set up a meeting with the Campbells in the land deed office.

"As soon as possible, and before winter sets in, for sure," he declared.

"Those greedy folks'll be drooling all over themselves at the sight of all that money," he said, smiling, as he sat down on his cot and began working at his boots.

"And, as for me, I'll be one step closer to Hettie."

CHAPTER 14

HARDSHIP

The Great Smoky Mountains
Late Fall 1838

One cold night while Hettie's family slept, huddled together around the fire-ring in the center of the cave, the first snow silently crept in and caught them by surprise. In all their years, neither Lame Bear nor Mattie Poor could remember having seen snow so soon.

It was at least two moons earlier than usual, coming almost at the end of summer, and even before the time they would have been celebrating the Purification Festival and the Green Corn Dance if they were still living at home.

A few days later an even worse blizzard struck, followed soon after by another, and then another. The wind howled almost continuously. Swirls of snow eddied under the door flap and muddied the floor of the cave. The drifts outside piled up one on top of the other until they reached almost to the level of the cave entrance.

Now Hettie and Sky complained because they were cold and there was nothing to do, even though Mattie Poor gave them plenty of chores. They emptied the slop bucket, swept out the cave, shoveled snow from the ledge into the kettle to melt for drinking water, shelled nuts, and spent hours and hours scraping and softening the hides of animals caught in the traps. Then they helped punch holes through the dried skins so that they could be laced and sewn together with their fish bone needles and thin strips of rawhide to make heavy clothing and warm bedding. Sky, especially, took pride in his work, and became highly skilled at scraping off every last speck of flesh.

The twins were acquiring new survival skills all the time, but there was such an unrelieved sameness to their lives that they were not often aware of it. They longed for the old life. And always, although the family no longer felt the need to be constantly vigilant, there was an ever-present, vague uneasiness and fear over being discovered.

Lame Bear spent hours making each member of the family a pair of snowshoes. He notched lengths of soaked river cane at regular intervals so that he could wind soft rawhide strips back and forth to make foot-shaped ovals. He then dried them slowly by the fire.

Now, even in the worst weather, they could perform their outdoor chores. Lame Bear, with Hettie at his side, was able to venture out regularly to check and reset the traps, scout for game, and look for evidence of soldiers.

Each hunting trip, however, seemed to take longer and longer and leave Lame Bear more and more exhausted. With only his blowgun and rope snares for weapons, he could never bring down large animals like deer and bear anymore and had to be satisfied with the smaller game.

He was catching fewer animals in his traps, too. Sometimes by the time he and Hettie had struggled over the surface of the deep icy snow, they would find that some hungry creature had gotten to the trap before them and already eaten the catch. More and more often, they returned home empty handed.

Mattie Poor could tell that Lame Bear was getting weaker. Lately, he seemed to cough and struggle for breath more and more, and she noticed that the shaking from his other sickness was back again. But still, he tried to help with the work in the cave just as he had back at the farm. Sometimes when he would be sitting cross-legged sharpening flint into points for the tips of his darts, he'd even talk about making a bow and a quirk of arrows like in the old days. If he could just remember how, he said.

Following the relative abundance of the warmer months, Mattie Poor began to dole out the food more and more sparingly. And after she caught Sky helping himself one day, she took to placing the provisions behind protective barricades of tools and firewood. Lame Bear called it her arsenal.

The intensive foraging for food and firewood over the summer, and the effort required to walk long distances with snowshoes, had turned Hettie's body lean and muscular. She was taller as well. She now stood eye to eye with Lame Bear and might even be a little taller. It was hard to tell, especially on days when he was more stooped than usual.

Hettie hadn't noticed before but her hair had also grown back nicely after her encounter with the brier patch. She was surprised to see that it was now as thick as Sky's. Each morning, she started spending a lot of time grooming their hair; first with the coarse wooden comb Lame Bear had carved for them, and then with clarified fat to make it smooth and glossy. Finally, she would replait their hair, usually giving each of them a single perfectly woven braid.

Sometimes if Mattie Poor was in a really good mood, she would let Hettie do her hair too. Hettie would kneel behind her, loosen the old braid, and gently pull apart the matted and snarled strands. With a slow, soothing rhythm, she would begin to comb and smooth, comb and smooth, until Mattie Poor's hair felt like wispy corn silk. Prolonging the physical contact with her grandmother brought back almost forgotten but comforting memories from long ago.

Both twins soon forgot what it was like to feel full after a meal. And even though winter had barely begun, Mattie Poor was already supplementing their food with pot scrubbers.

At first, after soaking them in water to soften them and to get rid of the worst of the bitter taste, she mixed them with more palatable food like rabbit or fish stew. Then she took to grinding them up into a powder and adding them along with the chestnuts to make the bread go farther. After a while, she even began giving them noonday meals of wild potato and pot scrubber's soup. When the potatoes were used up, pot scrubbers in broth was all they got for lunch, especially if they were planning to be inside that day.

Now and then, however, Lame Bear and Hettie, after long hours in the wind and cold, were able to bring home enough small game for a real meal. And sometimes, one of the traps would hold a beaver or raccoon that hadn't already been raked over. Then they would savor the bounty, bask in the warmth of the fire, and regain some of their strength.

CHAPTER 15

WHAT'S TWO OLD INDIANS, MORE OR LESS?

Rattlesnake Springs, Tennessee
Late Fall 1838

Ben had been happy when the first two removal parties, under General Winfield Scott's direction, had departed during the summer months because it helped to relieve the overcrowding in the stockade. Unfortunately, however, the detachments had almost immediately encountered unrelenting heat and unexpected severe drought.

The conductors of the parties found that most of the water holes they'd been counting on for the Cherokees and their livestock were completely dried up. In the end, they'd had to give up and return to camp. So now the people were just as miserable and crowded as before.

The stories coming back with them told of sickness and terrible suffering among the ill-prepared Indians. The sweltering conditions seemed to set the stage for the spread of contagious diseases, such as measles and cholera, which zigzagged their way up and down the boats and the wagon trains.

During the confusion on these first two journeys, Ben heard rumors that hundreds of Cherokees had managed to escape and were slowly finding their way back to the mountains of Georgia and Tennessee and into hiding.

To try to prevent any more deaths and to alleviate as much of the suffering as possible, Cherokee Chief John Ross had met with General Scott over the summer. Chief Ross had promised to take personal responsibility for the rest of the removal if General Scott would put off any more departures during the terrible heat of the summer. Scott had agreed to the postponement until fall in return for turning over the responsibility for the rest of the unpopular removal to the Cherokee leader himself.

But when September came and the removal parties started moving out again, this time with Chief John Ross in charge of the planning, reports soon filtered back that, instead of heat and drought, the groups were encountering unseasonable cold weather, heavy rains, and muddy, impassible trails. In these harsh conditions, Ben heard that many Cherokees were forced to sleep out in the open, most with only a thin blanket or sometimes with no blanket at all. And not everyone had moccasins or shoes, either.

"How did it get this cold so fast," he thought, shivering as he held onto the cuffs of his uniform sleeves with his fingers and wrestled them into his greatcoat before taking up his regular tour of duty in the camp. Even though the stinging black flies were gone and the smell from the latrine trenches less noticeable, the duty was just as abhorrent to him because the freezing temperatures only seemed to intensify the already miserable conditions inside. All the Cherokees were suffering and there were people dying almost daily. He felt powerless and frustrated, even though he and one of his fellow officers had established a regular routine of distributing all the leftover food they could find as well as any old discarded Army-issue wool blankets they could scrounge up.

Here it was only November and already cases of frostbite were being treated in the medical tent almost daily while off in the distance, Ben could see the mountains, unaware of the suffering around them, sleeping peacefully under their soft lavender covers.

The stockades and emigration depots were almost empty now. For the past two months, over two week intervals, the Army had been emptying them out, not just at Rattlesnake Springs, but all over Georgia, North Carolina, and Tennessee, a thousand or so Indians at a time.

He heard that the newspapers back East were full of dramatic and graphic stories of suffering, sickness, and death on this forced march soon dubbed The Trail of Tears. Congress was in an uproar. Famous people like Davy Crockett and Ralph Waldo Emerson were speaking out against it.

Each morning before he went on duty, he was drawn to the bulletin board in the officers' mess and carefully scanned the reports being sent back daily. The horrors they represented were almost unbearable to read, but he could not keep himself away.

He stood there and forced himself to count the cases of bloody flux, foot rot, frostbite, and pneumonia. He counted the number of births, the number of broken axles and lame oxen, the number of injured and sick who had to be left behind, to catch up when and if they could, the number of families who were forced to barter away their possessions to pay the outrageous tolls being levied by greedy landowners along the way, and, finally, the number of shallow graves that were being dug each day beside the trails.

So far, however, using one excuse after another, he had managed to keep Halfmoon and Gertrude's names, as well as his own, off each new relocation list. But now the headcount in the depot was down to less than two hundred. He knew that the last removal party was being formed now.

Chief John Ross, himself, with his wife Quatie at his side, was going to be a part of this last group of Cherokees. It was expected to be much less rigorous than the previous parties. The Cherokees assigned to this final detachment were said to be mainly old folks and others too sick or feeble to survive the hardships experienced by the previous removal parties. It was rumored that Mrs. Ross was one of the most frail and sickly of them all.

He realized that the old sisters' names would have to appear on this final roster. It couldn't be helped. He knew he'd run out of deferments and excuses.

"But, it won't matter," he told himself.

"I don't need any more delays. I'm about ready now. One more quick trip to Lame Bear's place and I'll be all set.

"If all goes according to plan," he said to himself, "Halfmoon and Gertrude won't be anywhere to be seen when that final roll call comes around. No sir! They'll be reported missing, sure, but who besides me is going to care?

"What's two old Indians, more or less, the captain'll most likely say. Why, I can just hear him. He'll probably just think they're already gone, anyway, shipped out by mistake with the Taylor or the Hildebrand Party.

"Why shucks, they'll be too darn busy trying to shut down this stinking hell hole to fret about a pair of harmless old Indians, anyway.

"Everybody knows Rattlesnake Springs and New Echota aren't much more than ghost towns now anyway, with only Army detachments and a few stragglers left. Why even the Cherokees' capital buildings, like the Council House and the Printing Office, stand empty now with the grass waist high and all.

"And once Chief Ross and his party's on its way," he reasoned, "if my plan works, there'll be nobody left in these parts to worry about anything, much less two harmless old ladies like Halfmoon and Gertrude.

"Nobody, that is, but me," he said, smiling to himself. "And my brother, Gabriel."

Now The Day is Over

"It's been reported that this household is still in possession of a hunting rifle, and under the law, the Cherokees are not permitted to own firearms."

CHAPTER 16

TOGETHER IN SONG

The Great Smoky Mountains
Winter 1838

When Lame Bear had finished the snowshoes for Hettie and Sky, he made them each a blowgun like his own. Using pebbles for practice instead of darts, they spent hours standing on the ledge out front aiming at the tree trunks below. Sky was the better shot. He would laugh whenever Hettie missed. It felt good to hear him.

But once their chores were done and blowgun practice over, the days continued to seem endless. Even Sky got sick of playing marbles. Hettie tried to invent new games they could both play and for a while that helped to pass the time, but the monotony of life in the dark smoky cave continued to hang over them.

Hettie longed for the old way of life. She wished she could attend school at the mission again and dreamed about someday having a family of her own. As she scraped the rotting flesh off a fox pelt, she thought about some of the young men she knew in Ellijay and New Echota and tried to picture what it would be like to join blankets with any of them.

Most of all, however, she thought about that evening last spring when Sergeant Stone had come to the cabin to take Lame Bear's rifle. She had realized at the time that he might be interested in her. And then that afternoon in the field when he'd helped her with the river cane, she'd been sure of it.

"I wonder if I'll ever see him again?" she asked herself.

"It's not that I like him or anything like that. How could I after what he and those others did to Halfmoon and Gertrude? Still, I wouldn't mind asking him a question or two. Like how come they arrested Halfmoon and Gertrude and the Pritchards and how come they let those Campbells take over our farm?"

Lately, she and Sky had both begun to look forward to the days when Lame Bear would decide it was time to check his traps, set out more rope snares, and hunt for small game. In the past, he had usually taken Hettie by herself but lately he seemed to be including Sky more and more often.

One of the reasons was that during the long empty days in the cave, Hettie had been teaching Sky a new set of hand signals especially for hunting and times of danger. With snow covering the ground, his footsteps in the snowshoes were muted anyhow but now he was also learning how to creep along silently, to stay close to Hettie and to watch carefully for her signs.

In the beginning, teaching him not to make noise was frustrating for them both. He just couldn't grasp the idea that the animals could hear him, and Hettie couldn't seem to get through to him. Finally, Mattie Poor, who had been observing her efforts, suggested that Hettie get Sky to put one of his hands against her throat and the other against his own.

When, for the first time, he felt the vibrations in her throat, he immediately recognized what they were. His beautiful face lit up, at first with shock and surprise, and then with a sudden understanding of how hearing people communicated with each other.

He took to wandering around the cave, two fingers resting lightly on his Adam's apple, making humming noises and experimenting with different physical sensations in his throat until Mattie Poor would eventually smack him on the back of the head.

"Enough, Sky, enough," she'd sign impatiently.

Sky, grinning, would tease her with one final raucous buzz before moving on to something else.

When they were out in the hills Hettie noticed, too, that he was beginning to be able to judge conditions for himself. Oftentimes he was able to anticipate her signals; she found she could depend upon him to maintain complete silence, to take cover quickly, and even to freeze in place.

Meanwhile, Lame Bear's health worried them all more and more. Some days were better than others, of course, but they could all see that he was steadily losing ground. Always quiet, he hardly spoke at all now and the trembling in his hands never seemed to let up. He could barely manage to eat or drink without spilling.

His complexion, lighter than Hettie and Sky's to begin with, recently had taken on a yellowish cast, and he was developing dark raccoon-like rings around his deep-set eyes. Sometimes he lay on his skins throughout the entire day without rising at all. When he did join them for a meal, he ate next to nothing.

The twins took to offering him sips of water throughout the day and at mealtimes took turns holding his bowl under his chin to keep him from wasting his food.

Mattie Poor studied him carefully and then dosed him with roots and powders from her special medicine pouch. Remembering the remedy for biliousness learned long ago from Kookowee, Halfmoon's *shaman* husband, she prepared a special tea made from the tender inside bark of the ash tree. She also talked to Hettie about fixing a steam treatment for him using six different kinds of firewood.

Hettie was used to seeing her father ailing but this clearly was not the same. She offered to help set up a makeshift *osi* and to go out and collect the special kinds of firewood needed. But Mattie Poor could not remember what they were, only that there were supposed to be six different kinds.

"I'll have to think on it for a while," Mattie Poor said to her as she brewed the tea.

"Maybe it'll come to me in the night while I'm sleeping. Meanwhile," she said, holding out the steaming cup, "this should make him feel better."

Hettie took the cup of ash bark tea over to her father and knelt down beside him. Holding the cup to his lips, she said,

"Here, drink some of this, Lame Bear, but watch out, it's very hot."

She paused while he took a sip.

"Winter will be over before you know it," she said reassuringly, "and you'll be your old self again, for sure, when spring comes.

"But until you're better, from now on, Sky and I want you to let us do the hunting and trapping by ourselves.

"Here, have some more tea," she said, gently wedging the rim of the cup between his cracked lips and slowly tipping it up.

"We're ready to take over, Lame Bear. We've watched you long enough and you've taught us well. You shouldn't have to go out anymore when it's so cold and you're feeling sick besides. Please let us do this, Lame Bear, please."

Slowly, Lame Bear replied, "This winter has been hard on all of us but especially on you, Hester. You should be with others your own age, getting ready for the time when you will be bringing a husband into the Wild Potato Clan, instead of being here in this cave taking care of me.

"But, you're right," he said. "You and Sky are ready to hunt and trap without me. There is always danger but I am no longer strong and for a long time I've had trouble keeping up. You and Sky must do it alone from now on."

Propped up on one elbow, he gestured towards the cup in her hand.

"More," he said.

Swallowing with difficulty, he closed his eyes and rested a moment before speaking again.

"When you hunt, there are two things you must always remember. This is what the old men told me when I was a boy.

"First you must always keep track of landmarks already there but also be sure to make your own blazes too, so you can find your way home. Do this even when you think you know the way.

"It's easy to get careless and trust your footprints to bring you back, but don't forget, they cannot help you in snows and rains or when darkness comes. Always remember that one small notch in a tree is better than a whole hillside of footprints."

The effort of speaking was taking its toll and Lame Bear began wheezing and gasping for breath. After resting and composing himself he was able to continue.

"The second thing to remember is to respect the land of our people and the wildlife on it. Take only what you need, and when you have hunted, give thanks to the animal for the food it provides you.

"Now, at first light, pack your moccasins tightly with dried grasses for warmth, fill your shoulder bags with darts and food, and cover yourselves with our thickest body skins and leggings. Go to the western slope first, especially that stand of trees beyond Turtle Rock and the waterfall, where we saw those rabbit tracks. Mattie and I'll be waiting for your return."

As instructed, Hettie and Sky set out early the next morning before any of the mist had burned off the mountain. Heading towards the western slope, Hettie pointed out the barely perceptible trail blazes that Lame Bear had already left, and when they changed direction, she signed to Sky to make notches of their own.

After several fruitless hours, Sky, who was taking his turn in the lead, stopped suddenly as he spotted some fresh rabbit tracks in the snow. He pointed to them with one mittened hand while holding the other against his throat to remind himself to keep silent. For some time, they followed the paw prints across the hills and valleys until, at last, they ended in the hollow trunk of a fallen tree.

Hettie signed for Sky to be the shooter. He took up a position on the hillside about ten paces above the bore, his dart gun at his lips, nodding to her when he was ready. She squatted down at the far end of the huge log and began to howl like a coyote, all the while beating on the bark with a stick.

Nothing happened. They waited expectantly. Still nothing. But, then, just as Sky relaxed his grip on his blowgun, the rabbit popped out. It landed on its haunches for just an instant, and then took off up the hill. Sky never even got off a shot.

Disappointed, they regrouped and started tracking it again. Their shadows became longer and longer against the hillside and they began to suffer from the intense cold. Their noses ran constantly. But still they continued on just as they knew Lame Bear would. At each turning, Sky was careful to cut a small blaze in a nearby tree while they both took note of the surroundings.

But the rabbit tracks just kept going and going. Their legs ached from the clumsy snowshoes and from the distances they'd traveled over the uneven terrain. Their fingers and toes were numb.

Finally, Hettie, who was leading by now, stopped and turned around to face Sky.

"We have to give up for today, Sky," she signed as she spoke.

"It's a long way back and we don't want to be caught out here after dark.

"Tomorrow or maybe the next day, we'll come back and set up a couple of snare traps," she said as she formed her fingers into a circle and then made a choking motion at her throat. "We'll catch him that way."

She tipped her head slightly towards the east and signed, "Home, now, dark soon."

Sky nodded in agreement and they turned towards home. No longer required to be quiet, he began to make his favorite repetitive buzzing noises. Hettie listened for a while and then started humming along trying to match her pitch to his.

At first it was just a game to her, but when their eerie chants began to meld together in strident harmony and ring out over the valley, she was suddenly overwhelmed.

She started to cry. This was the first time they had ever sung together and Sky didn't even realize they were doing it. As she led the way home, she sang and cried at the same time. For him, for her, and for their Nation.

Chapter 17

The Abduction

Rattlesnake Springs, Tennessee
Winter 1838

As expected, Ben found Halfmoon and Gertrude's names posted on the final relocation list. And, to his surprise, his own was there too. He had thought he was going to be assigned to closing down the emigration depot, but, instead, they had listed him as a military escort for the removal party, set to move out on December 4th, just three days hence.

This final group, the thirteenth, would include Chief John Ross, his wife Quatie, and their children. The directive on the bulletin board stated that the removal party would assemble at nearby Ross's Landing, travel north past Nashville, cross over the Cumberland Mountains into Kentucky where they'd turn westward. When they reached the Mississippi River, they'd ferry across to Cape Girardeau in Missouri and follow the Greensferry Road towards Rollo and Springfield where they'd turn southwest toward Fort Smith. After crossing the Arkansas River, their final destination would be Fort Gibson in Indian Territory.

"Just barely time enough to go home and get Gabriel and the wagon before I have to head out," he thought to himself as he blew on his fingers and stamped his feet against the cold.

Sadly, he realized he wouldn't be able to find Hettie before he left. He knew, though, that he was very close to locating her. He had narrowed his search to two hunting caves he knew about. The most likely one, about a half-day north of Lame Bear's place, was near a waterfall and an outcropping of rocks the Cherokees called Turtle Rock. The second cave was farther away on Rich Mountain and it had been years since he'd been up there. He remembered, however, that both caves were so well hidden he and his brother Gabriel hadn't even known they were there until their father had pointed them out.

Now, with these new orders, he'd run out of time. He'd just have to hope and pray that the family would be all right until spring. From what he could understand, he should be able to make it back by then. But, for now, he'd have to leave everything else in Gabriel's hands.

During his last trip home to Dalton, his parents had given Gabriel permission to stay with Halfmoon and Gertrude on Lame Bear's farm north of Ellijay until spring planting time, even though they weren't absolutely convinced he was ready for so much responsibility. Now, Ben wasn't so sure either.

"Me being gone wasn't part of the bargain," he thought, "although we always knew it might happen. I can't help wondering, though, how Maw and Paw will feel now. After all, Gabriel's only sixteen years old."

Suddenly, he was filled with anxiety. So much was at stake. He wondered if he was doing the right thing. Most of all, he wished he could find out if Hettie was safe before he had to leave. He longed to be with her. There was so much he wanted to tell her and so much more he wanted to find out about her. Now, it was too late.

The next day after completing his morning report, he signed out, saddled Sonny, and headed for home. Light, powdery snow was beginning to fall as he set off on the gravel road. He thought about Halfmoon and Gertrude, out in the open, huddled together against the bitter cold.

He was sure they'd never be able to survive the trek west. What they were going through right now at the depot was bad enough. He knew that many of the Cherokees taking sick and dying almost daily out on the trail weren't even as old as Halfmoon and Gertrude.

"But, still, I got to admit, those two old birds turned out to be a lot tougher than I ever thought, that's for sure," he said to himself as he watched Sonny flatten his ears whenever the intermittent snowflakes touched down on his head and shaggy mane and melted from his warmth.

Ben reached home late that afternoon, as it was growing dark. Together he and Gabriel unsaddled Sonny and dried him off. After bedding him down in the barn, they lowered their heads against the swirling snow and made their way across the yard to the warmth of the farmhouse.

When supper was over, the family sat close together in front of the fireplace, staring into the glowing embers while Ben and Gabriel slowly and carefully reviewed their plans for abducting Halfmoon and Gertrude from the emigration depot the next day.

Very early the following morning, they loaded the tools and supplies that Gabriel would need for his stay at Lame Bear's place above Ellijay into the farm wagon, hitched up Sadie, and then saddled Sonny. Together they checked off the items on their list and then also made sure they'd left enough room in the back of the wagon for their two passengers. Finally they covered the load with a brittle old oilskin.

Ben thanked his parents again for agreeing to help two old Indians they didn't even know. As he said his goodbyes, his eyes welled up at the sight of them standing there, side by side. He took a deep breath, blinked hard, and tried to focus over their heads on the bare branches of the chestnut tree until he was in control again. Then he stepped back and saluted them.

He had agreed to drive Sadie and the wagon so Gabriel could ride Sonny. Now the boy was impatient to be on the road. They made arrangements to meet again at Ridge's Rock just outside Rattlesnake Springs.

Sonny sensed the excitement and tension in the air and when Gabriel tapped him with his heels, he responded by arching his neck and lifting his hooves smartly in his best parade-ground style.

Ben untied Sadie's reins from the tree and climbed up on the wooden seat of the farm wagon. The round little mule, resigned to another day of work, started off at her own pace, steady and deliberate as always.

Gabriel was quickly out of sight, but the slow progress of the mule suited Ben just fine. It gave him a chance to go over the details of his plan one last time. He needed to make sure everything was in place. While he sat on the cracked board with Sadie's reins looped loosely around his wrist, he wondered if he would have gone to all this trouble with Halfmoon and Gertrude if Hettie had not been in the picture.

With or without her, he decided, he could never let those two old people start off on a journey that would almost surely be the death of them. How could he do that? He was just sorry he hadn't been able to do more to help at the depot.

He regretted too that he hadn't found Hettie's hiding place. But if he was right about where they were, he felt almost certain they'd be safe until he could get back from the west. Especially now that Tsali, the Cherokee also known as Old Charley, who they said had killed a soldier trying to bring him in, had been recaptured. After Tsali had been executed by a firing squad in November, General Scott had kept his word and the Army was no longer hunting down the other Cherokees still hiding in the mountains.

Still, he wished he could see Hettie before he left, to tell her she didn't have to be afraid anymore. He longed to be able to tell her how sorry he was for taking part in the removal and to let her know how much he cared for her. She didn't know any of this yet.

Plodding along contentedly, Sadie reached Ridge's Rock in her own good time. Gabriel, who'd arrived much earlier, had dismounted, loosened Sonny's girth, and was drowsing in the winter sun on top of the smooth rock, daydreaming and listening to the rhythmic tearing sounds that the horse's big teeth made as he foraged for tufts of grass. Gabriel had already jumped down to the ground to wait for them because he'd heard Sadie's familiar high, nasal whinnies to Sonny long before they came into view.

The brothers, one muscular and well developed, the other still gangly and awkward, stood talking quietly in the middle of the road, and then Gabriel hoisted himself up and over the side of the buckboard and untied the reins. He clicked the tip of his tongue against the roof of his mouth until Sadie, who'd found some of that tender grass for herself, reluctantly took up her mission again.

Sonny, bored now, and in a hurry to get back to the hay and oats that he knew were waiting for him in his stall not far down the road, champed at the bit. He began to mark time impatiently with his hooves as he shook his head from side to side, scattering frothy bits of green foam into the frosty air around his brown velvet muzzle.

When Ben reached headquarters at Rattlesnake Springs, the private in charge of the stables came forward, saluted, and accepted Sonny's reins. After giving directions for the horse's care, Ben turned and walked rapidly towards his tiny, drafty quarters.

Throwing off his cumbersome greatcoat, he took out his document case and removed the precious deed to the property, which had once been Lame Bear's and now belonged to him. The Campbells, back on their original old rundown place outside Rome, Georgia, had been only too happy to sell it to him two months ago.

He placed the deed carefully to one side and sat down at his desk. Reaching under the edge of the leather blotter holder, he retrieved the envelope and one of the two sheets of parchment paper he'd bought at the store next to the courthouse.

He fitted a shiny new nib into the tip of his pen and lifted the top of the built-in inkwell on the desk. Solemnly, he dipped the pen up and down. After soaking up the excess ink with his new green felt wiper, he used his best grammar school penmanship to begin copying the example of a habitation permit the county clerk had written out for him.

> *To Whom It May Concern,*
>
> *I, Benjamin Stone, 2nd Lieutenant, U.S. Army Infantry, do hereby give permission for my brother, Gabriel Stone, minor son of Jacob and Rebecca Stone of Dalton, Georgia, to inhabit my homestead north of Ellijay, Georgia along with Halfmoon and Gertrude, last names unknown.*
> *The deed to this homestead is attached. I, Benjamin Stone purchased it free and clear on October 3rd, 1838 from Obadiah Campbell, presently residing at Rome, Georgia.*
>
> *(Signed)*
> *Benjamin Stone*
> *December 3rd, 1838*

He blew gently on the parchment, lightly sanded it, and after a final inspection, lined up the letter and the deed, folded them in thirds, and placed them into the matching envelope which he slid carefully into his vest pocket.

Gripping the cuffs of his uniform blouse with the tips of his fingers, he jiggled back into his overcoat, and went outside to look down the road to make sure Gabriel was at the appointed spot under the oak tree. He and Sadie were just pulling up. They exchanged hand signals and Ben quickly turned and headed for the emigration depot.

He found a hub of activity and confusion inside the camp as the remaining detainees were being readied for the start of the journey the following morning. Piles of new blankets and food rations were being passed out but some of the Cherokees believed that accepting them would be construed as payment for their stolen lands and were refusing them. The supply sergeant was arguing with them, trying to explain how much they would be needed on the trail. Other soldiers were walking around with lists and inventories, calling out names, and shouting to each other.

At first Benjamin couldn't find Halfmoon and Gertrude. His heart sank. But then he recognized their unmistakable profiles framed against the uneven pales on the far side of the depot. The wind was whipping their skirts into a frenzy around their legs, but they were standing obediently, one in front of the other, in the supply sergeant's ragtag line.

He was so relieved to see them that, without realizing it, he broke into a trot as he crossed the nearly empty quadrangle.

He took a deep breath. Now he had to get them out of here without creating a ruckus. He hoped he could pull it off.

"Miss Gertrude, Miss Halfmoon," he called out in a loud voice as he approached them.

"How are you ladies today? Sorry to disturb you but the medical officer is waiting. Says he wants to see the both of you right away."

He hated having to trick them but he knew they'd never come willingly.

He took hold of Gertrude's arm and tried to direct her towards the gate. She stiffened at his touch.

"Excuse me, Ma'am, but we need to go," he said firmly. And then, when she didn't budge, more urgently. "Right away, Ma'am!"

Turning to Halfmoon, he added, "And you, too, Ma'am."

Wresting their baskets from them, he said smoothly, "Here, let me help you."

He turned his back, ignoring their startled protests and outstretched arms, and strode purposefully towards the gate, a basket in each hand. He expected them to hurry along behind him, concerned for their belongings, and when he was halfway across the compound, a quick sideways glance confirmed this.

The guard saluted him as he neared the gate. Switching both baskets to his left hand, he returned the salute and indicated with a tilt of his head and a shrug of his shoulder that he was responsible for the two women scurrying along behind him.

Once outside the gate, he turned onto the road toward the prearranged spot where Gabriel was waiting. As the three of them approached, the boy jumped down and quickly folded back the crackled old oilskin.

"Hurry now, get in." Benjamin ordered, as he shoved the baskets Halfmoon and Gertrude were still struggling to recover into the corner of the wagon. "I'll explain everything in a minute."

Quickly, in one continuous motion, he and Gabriel took hold of each loudly objecting woman by her elbows and swung her like a bale of hay into the back of the wagon. Ben hoisted himself in after them and held the stunned, struggling women firmly in place. Gabriel, meanwhile, raced around to the front, jumped up onto the seat and clucked at Sadie.

"Be quiet Ma'am," Ben ordered in a firm, low voice. "I'll explain everything as soon as we're out of town."

A short time later he began his story, starting with the apology they'd heard before and then quickly moving on to his love for Hettie, his purchase of Lame

Bear's property, and his intention to turn it over to Hettie and her family as soon as they could be found. In the meantime, he explained, his brother Gabriel would stay with them in Lame Bear and Mattie Poor's house so that they would be spared the relocation to the Reservation.

"You'll be safe here for the rest of your lives," he said, placing his hand over his heart. "I promise you."

He took out the thick envelope from his pocket and handed it to Halfmoon.

"This is the legal title for the cabin and the land and gives you permission to stay there."

"I hope that before too long Lame Bear and the others will be joining you.

"I have to get back to the emigration depot right away and I won't be seeing you for a long time, but my brother Gabriel here will help you. You'll be safe with him until I get back. And when I do return, I promise I'll look after you for the rest of your lives."

He signaled to Gabriel. Sadie slowed down and he jumped out. Standing alone in the center of the deserted road, he watched the wagon lurch away and slowly recede into the distance. He waved.

He watched Sadie mince along with her precious cargo. He couldn't believe it. All the planning had paid off and everything had gone like clockwork. It really looked like Gertrude and Halfmoon were going to be safe, even if they couldn't have their own property back.

Just before the little party disappeared around the bend, he saw Gertrude tentatively raise her hand in response to his wave, and, at the last possible moment, he thought he might have seen Halfmoon wave too.

He felt the mantle of guilt begin to slide a bit, and, as he turned back to the depot, he was filled with excitement and hope.

"It's only a beginning, I know, but glory be, what a beginning!"

CHAPTER 18

THE LONG WALK

The Great Smoky Mountains
Winter 1838

Mattie Poor had a savory stew of jerked beaver and hickory nuts simmering over the fire when Hettie and Sky returned. If she was disappointed that they were empty handed, she didn't show it. Lame Bear was asleep on his skins curled up next to the fire with a cup of his special ash bark tea at his side.

They placed their blowguns flat on the dirt floor before peeling off their wet furs and leggings and spreading them to dry. Shivering, they wrapped their thin bodies in their tattered old blankets and sidestepped awkwardly over to the fire.

Mattie Poor ladled out the steaming stew into the rough fire-blackened bowls she had made from river clay last summer to take the place of the enamelware they had left behind. Sky sat down and went right to work slurping noisily from his bowl, letting rivulets of grease ooze down his chin and dribble onto his blanket.

Hettie was just as tired and hungry as he was. She would have liked to gulp hers down too, but something held her back. Perhaps it was the memory of an incident that happened long ago.

She and Sky had been passing by Moogan's still with a wheelbarrow full of squash to share with Halfmoon and Gertrude, when a voice had boomed out from behind the sugar maple trees.

"Hey, you there, little savage girl, yeah you! Come on over here. Leave the dummy there. What I got is only for you. Come see what it is! You'll like it! You hear me? Come on over little savage girl, I'm waiting."

She was not a savage. She was absolutely sure about that. She knew herself to be a quiet girl, a serious girl, and a girl with dignity.

No, she was not a savage, she thought, and what's more, Sky was no dummy either. Yes, it was true that he couldn't hear or speak, and yes, she had to admit that sometimes he was a little slow besides, but for sure, he was no dummy.

She looked over at him. "Why, he can do lots of things better than me."

But, nevertheless, the cutting words of long ago still stung, and she was not able to forget them.

She wondered why the whites hated the Cherokees so much and why they treated them so badly. Was it because of all the gold that had been found in Dahlonega?

"If that's what they're after, they're welcome to it," she said to herself as she remembered the Campbells and all those holes they'd dug.

"Just so they leave us alone. All I really want, anyway, is our own place back, and maybe my blue gingham dress with the puffed petal sleeves that I only got to wear that one time.

"And, oh yes, I'd sure like to see Benjamin Stone again to hear him try to explain why they were so mean to Halfmoon and Gertrude. Yes, I'd like that. For sure."

She thought about the blue gingham dress and how it made her feel that day last fall when the Council began its three-day session. Mattie Poor, straight and tall as usual, was seated with the other Beloved Women, the *ghighaus*, right up front by the Eternal Flame with its seven sacred woods, one for each clan

"And I got to sit right behind them in the Wild Potato Clan section," she said. "I know I wasn't the prettiest girl there that day but I did look nice in my dress, and, for sure, I was the proudest. Not everybody has a Beloved Woman for a grandmother."

But right now, tired as she was, she was still proud because, in spite of Lame Bear's sickness, and all the other dangers and obstacles they'd faced, her family was surviving this first hard winter in the cave, thanks in large part, she realized, to Mattie Poor's planning and Lame Bear's cleverness.

She promised herself she'd never give in, never, and someday, somehow, she'd find a way to get their farm back from the Campbells.

Out loud, she said to Mattie Poor, "Just because we live in a cave right now doesn't make us savages and it doesn't mean we have to act that way, either. But just look at how Sky is eating, will you? Isn't that awful?"

She was already stiff and sore, but she forced herself to stand up. Clutching the corners of her blanket in her fist, she sidled over to where Mattie Poor was sitting. With her free hand, she reached onto the rock behind Mattie Poor and picked out two wooden spoons. She turned and handed one to Sky.

Over his head, she and Mattie Poor locked eyes for just an instant and she saw approval and admiration written all over the old woman's face. She wondered how much else Mattie Poor understood about her feelings. Would she tell her that it was useless to dream? That they could never go back?

But Mattie Poor told her none of those things. Instead she said,

"Tomorrow at first light Hester, you and Sky can go and check Lame Bear's traps for him. It's been three days now and when I made the stew today I thought to take some of the jerked meat that was spoiling and set it to softening for you. It's over there," she said, pointing, "next to the bait pouch."

After cleaning up, Mattie Poor banked the coals, checked on Lame Bear, got their fur pallets from the pile in the corner, and spread them out beside the fire.

Hettie lay down on her back, luxuriating in the lushness of the fur, and watched the spirals of tiny sparks bounce against the jagged ceiling of the cave where they mixed with the reflections of the darting red and orange tongues of fire. Very soon, however, the colors faded to just a few faint shadows and then, finally, to nothing more than an occasional flickering glow.

Lame Bear waited on his pallet until he heard the slow, regular breathing of the others as they drifted off, one by one. Cautiously, he opened his eyes and scrutinized the three sleeping forms. Satisfied, he sat up, drank the last of his ash bark tea, and, trying not to wheeze, slowly pulled out his fur leggings, moccasins, and mittens from under his blanket where he'd hidden them earlier in the day.

He crept slowly and almost silently on his hands and knees over to the mouth of the cave, dragging his clothing behind him. With much effort, he rose. Leaning on the wall, he put on his leggings, and tied his moccasins onto his gnarled and twisted feet. Holding his thin, worn blanket around his shoulders with one hand and his snowshoes and mittens with the other, he pushed aside the door flap and stepped out onto the ledge.

The air was heavy and still and his first breath shocked him. It was so cold it numbed his lungs and momentarily deadened his pain. He took his time climbing down, careful to avoid setting off any loose rocks or gravel that might give him away.

At the bottom, he paused to get his bearings and put on his mittens. After retrieving his walking stick from its hiding place, he dropped his snowshoes onto the ground and stepped into them. Drawing himself as upright as possible, he studied the sky.

The moon was a bright sliver of gold and the array of stars was so vast that, at first, he was dazzled and confused by their profusion. He felt light-headed and dizzy from the exertion of climbing down and every movement sent a new wave of agony though his body.

He knew he was weak and the distance great but he'd sensed that his last sleep was very close and he wanted to take his place near Sweetwater and the members of his first family. Above all, he didn't want to be a burden to Mattie and the twins any longer.

And so, using his walking stick for support, he began to painfully force one foot in front of the other. He maintained a slow but steady pace, using the descending stream to guide him. Sometimes he would slip on the ice and snow or his legs would buckle unexpectedly but the stick always managed to save him. He knew that if he fell, he might not be able to get up again. Because of the extreme cold, he knew too that there could be no resting tonight. And so he kept going, and going, and going.

While he labored on, he thought of Mattie and the twins sleeping back in the cave. He thought of long ago when Sweetwater used to stand by the doorway on nice days grinding corn in the *kanona*, of the way she rested her forehead against the cow's flank as she milked her, of how her skirt rode up in the back when she bent over to tend the beans and squash. He thought of all the cold nights when she used to press up against him in their rope and straw bed, careful not to wake Mattie. And he struggled on.

Towards morning, he sensed that the graveyard, his destination, was not far off. In a little while, he would be there. Soon, however, instead of inhaling stark cold whiteness with each raspy breath, he began to detect the faint but unmistakably rich aroma of a wood fire.

He stopped and tried to figure out where it was coming from. Was it other Cherokees in hiding, soldiers on patrol looking for them, white poachers, the Campbells? Who?

As he limped along, off in the distance he caught sight of a column of smoke. It started out sooty and thick on the horizon and gradually uncoiled itself into wispy gray puffs as it drifted upwards and streaked the sky. When he finally reached the clearing at the edge of the old apple orchard, he was surprised to discover that it was coming from his own chimney.

He stopped for a moment, leaning on his stick as he gasped for breath, and tried to puzzle out the scene in front of him. The half-burned pile of rubble from the Campbells was gone, and, in its place, the long morning light was casting shimmering shadows of gold over the clean white snow that encircled the house of his mother.

Just then the cabin door opened and a familiar old figure appeared, wrapped in a shawl, water bucket in hand. Taking her time, she stepped gingerly over the threshold, and began to shuffle towards the well.

"Halfmoon, is that you?" he croaked.

With his fur mitten, he broke off the jagged icicles hanging from his nostrils and began to stumble across the frozen field.

"Is that really you, Halfmoon?"

The Roundup Begins

Single file, the little family began its journey into hiding.

Chapter 19

The Trail Where We Cried

Ross's Landing, Tennessee
Winter 1838–1839

At first, it wasn't too bad. Benjamin could almost imagine that the Cherokees milling around the ferry dock at Ross's Landing were there of their own free will, getting ready for an early December river excursion instead of preparing for a forced march.

Now that he'd taken care of Halfmoon and Gertrude, he felt he could concentrate on his new assignment. He knew it was an honor to be named to the escort detail for the Chief of the Cherokees, John Ross, and his wife Quatie. The respected couple had arrived a short time ago, along with a small cluster of well-wishers to see them off.

Even though Chief Ross was a short, slight man, he had a distinguished way of carrying himself. Benjamin had been able to pick him out right away. During a lull in the loading activity, he stepped forward and saluted.

"Benjamin Stone, 2nd Lieutenant, United States Army, at your service, Sir. Here to provide escort for you and your family and to be of assistance in any way I can, Sir."

Ross was dressed in formal clothing with a high, stiff white collar, which almost touched the lobes of his large ears. He had a full head of graying hair neatly parted on one side. Ben was startled, however, by Ross' piercing pale blue eyes, which were intently scrutinizing him from underneath great, bushy eyebrows.

He stood at attention until Chief Ross put his hand on his wife Quatie's shoulder and gently drew her forward to introduce Ben to her.

"How do you do, Ma'am." he said, gingerly accepting the delicate hand she extended.

"I'm honored to be your escort, Ma'am, and hope I can be of service to you."

Smiling warmly, she said, "Thank you Lieutenant," and beckoned to two young boys who were playing nearby on the loading platform.

"Silas and George, this is Lieutenant Stone, who will be looking out for us," she said as Ben shook hands with them.

"Two of our older children, Jane and Allen, will be joining us shortly," she said.

As he walked back to take his place next to his knapsack, it suddenly came to him.

"I remember now. She's a full-blooded Cherokee but he's not. Not even half, hear tell, which explains those blue eyes. What's more, they say he was raised white too. Sure looks white to me. Maybe that's why they call him White Bird although there's probably a lot more to it than that."

He leaned back against the piling, propping one foot behind him for balance, and folding his arms across his chest to wait for the loading to be finished. Sonny was already safely on board one of the flatboats. Benjamin could see him bobbing his head and impatiently stamping one front hoof against the wooden planking. It was obvious he didn't like being tethered with the oxen and mules.

Ben watched as Chief Ross quietly and efficiently supervised the loading of his trunks and hampers, which contained the official documents and relics of the Cherokee Nation. He overheard someone say that Ross had letters between the Nation and every president going all the way back to George Washington himself. There were supposed to be sacred old beaded wampum belts in there too, handed down from when the Cherokees made peace with the Iroquois over two hundred years ago.

Every now and then Ross would interrupt his work for another sad goodbye. His wife, Quatie, her face almost hidden in the shadows of her wide brimmed bonnet, stood quietly behind him, with Silas and George never far away.

When everything was loaded to his satisfaction, the whistle blew and the Ross family boarded. The ferry with the flatboats in tow began to churn out from the landing. Ross and his wife stood leaning against the railing. Every once in a while they would wave to the people left on shore.

Suddenly the wind let out a long, shrill howl, and the sun disappeared behind the clouds. In the semi-darkness, it was hard to recognize anyone on the shore. As the cold became more noticeable, John and Quatie Ross stepped back from the railing, turned, and made their way inside. Even from his position next to Sonny on the flatboat, Benjamin could see that Mrs. Ross was shivering and looked frail. Perhaps the weight of her oversized dark cloak was too much for her.

Once across the river, the ferry, its work done, discharged its load of passengers, animals, and wagons. The removal party regrouped under the direction of John Ross and the other leaders. For a short distance, they traveled on the well-maintained Federal Road before cutting over to the worn trails that would carry them northwest through Tennessee, Kentucky, and the lower edge of Illinois, and then in a southwesterly direction across Missouri and Arkansas until they reached the Cherokee Reservation in the west.

Early on, Chief Ross and the party's conductor had developed a daily routine. At first light, they would send an advance team ahead to the next night's campsite to make sure there would be water and provisions for the party. Then with both leaders on horseback, the two of them, along with the wagon master, Mr. Dudley, would spend the day riding back and forth along the lines, overseeing, and helping out wherever they could.

During the course of each day's march, the Cherokees gradually sorted themselves out until the wagon train eventually stretched over several miles, with the riders and the strong walkers at the front, the wagons, carts, and carriages in the middle, and the mothers with children, the elderly, and the sick struggling along at the rear.

As early as the second day, Benjamin sensed that this removal party was going to be no easier than any of the others that had gone before. He was afraid for the Cherokees in his group. They seemed so ill prepared for the terrible hardships that he sensed lay ahead. Only a few possessed the proper clothing and tents to protect themselves from the cold, wet conditions, and, moreover, almost all of them already appeared to be malnourished and weakened from the months of deprivation and inactivity in the stockades and emigration depots. The weather, usually fairly tolerable in December, was already turning bitter cold and the journey had only just begun.

He knew that if he was going to be of any real help to these people in the coming days, weeks, and perhaps even months, he needed to become more involved than just as a military escort. He felt there was no time to lose. He also recognized, however, that he must use extreme care in whatever he decided to do so that neither the conductor nor Chief Ross would look at his efforts as interference. He was already ashamed of the behavior of some of his fellow military escorts who openly made fun of the Cherokees' ways but still tried to take advantage of the young women every chance they got and he knew that the Cherokee leaders resented their presence on the march.

Ben found his opening on the third evening of the march when he observed exhausted stragglers dragging into camp long after most of the others were already starting their cooking fires. When he was done helping them collect their daily rations from the quartermaster and set up their pitifully inadequate shelters, he walked over to where he saw Chief Ross conferring with Mr. Dudley, the wagon master. He waited, respectfully, a short distance away, for a chance to speak.

"Sir," he said, stepping forward, as Ross acknowledged him. "I'd like to volunteer for duty at the rear of the line. There's a need back there to see that no one gets lost or lags behind. With your permission, Sir."

After thinking it over for a moment, Ross spoke.

"That seems like a good idea, Lieutenant. At least we'll try it for the next few days and see how it goes.

"You can start tomorrow morning. See that you report daily to Mr. Dudley here with a list of injuries, sickness, breakdowns, and the like.

"And, oh yes, another thing," Ross said. "While you're at it, keep a sharp eye out for those whiskey peddlers we've seen sneaking around back there, trying to sell their poison to our people."

Consequently, Ben started spending his days working at the end of the line and now he and Sonny were among the last to reach the campgrounds each evening. Sometimes he would be riding double and sometimes he would be on foot with someone else on Sonny's back.

In the mornings, he and Sonny would be among the last to pull up stakes, too, even though Benjamin would have been up at the break of day lending a hand with the loading of the wagons and the hitching up of the teams. He always felt better when he knew that everyone else was safely underway before starting off himself.

At first, the trail seemed fairly passable, at least as far as McMinnville. Soon thereafter, however, the party's progress was slowed by thick, soupy mud, which filled and hid the deep ruts left by all the wagons that had gone before. The oxen and mules began having trouble with this treacherous footing as well as with the increasingly slippery inclines.

Broken axles and bent wheels became a daily occurrence and both the wagon master and the smithy were kept busy far into the night. One family had already been left behind to wait for replacement parts when their wagon couldn't be repaired overnight.

One evening, within sight of Oaklands Mansion on the outskirts of Murfreesboro, Tennessee, after most of the party had stopped for the night, Ben, bringing up the rear as usual, rode into camp with a tired little boy clinging to the saddle horn in front of him. He was surprised to see a small group of obviously distressed strangers collapsed beside the trail. He learned they were from the removal party ahead of them, which should have been at least two weeks further down the trail. The weaker Cherokees in that group had fallen behind, a little more each day, until, now, Chief Ross's' detachment had overtaken them.

As he rode by, he saw that some of them were suffering from the bloody flux as well as other painful ailments, including one poor soul with gangrene. They were a troubling sight and his heart went out to them even as his stomach retched at the foul odors from their feces and pus.

Each evening, he spotted more and more of these exhausted Cherokees as he accompanied the last of his own marchers into camp, until by the time they'd crossed into Kentucky it was hard to tell where the previous removal party left off and Ross's began.

A few miles past the Kentucky border they came to a campground near a town called Hopkinsville. Here, John Ross and the other leaders paused at the graves of the great warrior, Chief Whitepath, and another Cherokee leader named Fly Smith. The elderly pair had been in one of the earlier removal parties and had been among the first to sicken and die on the trail. As they passed by, Ben noticed that many of the Cherokees placed small stones, feathers, and other keepsakes on the graves.

The intermittent rains, at first just a nagging annoyance, soon became insistent and life threatening. At night the rain often turned into icy sleet, which reached its merciless, chilling fingers into shawls, and moccasins, and under blankets that were already too thin. Sometimes, at the end of the long day, it was nearly impossible for many of the families to keep a fire going long enough to cook the meager salt pork and often-wormy cornmeal handed out by the quartermaster at each stopping point. Ben noticed that the cornmeal served to him and the other escorts never seemed to have that problem, however.

Pulling and pushing wagons and carriages up and over the mountains became a nightmare. The horses, mules, and oxen strained again and again to gain traction in the slippery mud and became worn out in their efforts. Sometimes it took several teams and many men to get a single wagon up and over a bad place. And then the struggle would begin all over again with the next wagon.

At night, after camp had been made, Benjamin, tired as he was, volunteered again, this time to help Dr. Powell, the party's painfully thin and stooped physician. In the beginning, John Ross's wife, Quatie, had assisted Dr. Powell, especially with the women and children, but after only a few days she had become too ill herself and now could scarcely leave her own pallet once camp had been made.

So, after seeing that Sonny was watered, fed and hobbled out of the wind, Ben would carry the bulky medical supplies from one campfire to another as the kindly old man with the palsied hands ministered to the sick.

Ben was surprised to see that many of the doctor's medicines and treatments, like willow bark and dried foxglove leaves, were the same ones his grandmother and mother had used when he was growing up. Becoming more confident each evening, he soon found himself anticipating the doctor's needs, handing him his instruments and helping to administer medicines.

One evening, they came across an old man named Jesse Birdsong lying on his side next to the trail with his family in a silent semi-circle around him. The Cherokee's breathing was labored and a steady trickle of phlegm was oozing from his mouth and dribbling in stringy yellow threads down his chin.

After setting down the heavy field knapsack and instrument bag he had been carrying, Benjamin stepped back out of the way. He watched the doctor kneel down, screw the pieces of his wooden stethoscope together and, positioning the bell-shaped end against the old man's chest, listened intently for breath sounds.

"It's pneumonia, alright," the doctor announced.

"Here," he said, handing Ben the hollow wooden tube. "Have a listen."

Ben crouched down and took the stethoscope as Dr. Powell guided his hand to key points on the man's chest.

"There," he said. "Hear those crackles and rales down there? And there? There too, and, now, up here, can you hear his heartbeat? Move it around yourself until you pick up that flub-a-dub."

As Ben leaned forward and listened intently, a look of astonishment and wonder came over his face upon hearing the sound of Jesse Birdsong's beating heart.

"Nothing like it, is there, Boy?" the doctor said as he reached back into his bag for the bottle of calomel. He shook it, and then uncorked it, using his sleeve to clean off the rim. Then in one continuous motion, he braced the old man's lips open with the trembling fingers of his other hand and quickly poured a generous dose of calomel straight from the bottle down his throat.

Turning to Benjamin as he recorked the bottle, he said,

"See if you can make room for this man in the medical wagon. Once he's settled, I'll come and mix up a mustard poultice for him. That's about all we can do for him tonight."

"Sir, I know how to fix one of those," Benjamin said. "In fact, my chest is still smarting from all the mustard my Grandma used to lay on me before I was big enough to fight back!"

Dr. Powell laughed. "Then, go ahead, young man," he said, "by all means. You'll most likely find some pre-measured mustard seed packets in the wagon but take one or two out of my bag anyway just to be on the safe side. There's an extra stethoscope in there for you to use too. Leave the poultice on for as long as he can stand it, the longer the better, at least a quarter-hour anyhow.

"Now, then, where's that child got his foot run over this afternoon?"

Benjamin, with the help of Birdie's family, carried him on his blanket back to the wagon. He took out a paper of the powdered black mustard and sprinkled it into an old shaving mug he found in a supply box in the wagon. Then he went to a family camping nearby and asked for hot water. He poured it into his cup, a little at a time, and stirred it until he had a nice thick paste. Lifting a square of old petticoat flannel from the same box, he spread the already pungent mixture evenly over its soft surface while Birdsong's family watched suspiciously.

Folding it carefully, as he'd seen his grandmother do, so that none of the mustard would ooze out and burn the old man's skin, he squatted down next to his patient. Between gasps, Birdsong was babbling on about looking for some lost tribe and hardly noticed when Benjamin bared his chest and tied on the flannel.

Satisfied, Ben settled back on his heels to wait for the mustard to work its magic.

He could hear someone down the line playing a mouth organ. He recognized a haunting refrain that lately had been making the rounds of the barracks. Resting his head against a wooden stave supporting the canvas siding on the side of the wagon, he began to softly hum along with the sweet, tinny notes.

Be it ever so humble,
There's no place like home!
Home, home, sweet home,
There's no place like home.

He must have dozed off because gradually he began to make out Hettie's face. She looked even more grown-up now than she had in his dream. Her face was thinner and her eyes more thoughtful and solemn. But, nevertheless, she was looking up at him with a loving smile and calling out to him,

"Home, home, Benjamin, come home, come home."

But, suddenly, instead of Hettie, he realized it was Old Birdie crying out to him. He was struggling to sit up and clawing at the stinging plaster on his chest.

Startled, and then embarrassed, Ben lunged forward and quickly untied it, apologizing for his inattention. After he'd settled the old man back down for the night, he had another listen to his chest with the doc's second best stethoscope. He thought he heard fewer rales this time. In fact, he was sure he did.

Backing out of the wagon to go tell Dr. Powell, he was surprised to see the doctor's big bay tied across the way alongside the Ross family's tent.

"She must be even worse tonight," Benjamin thought as he decided to wait in case he was needed again.

A short time later, Dr. Powell poked his head out of the tent. Spotting Ben, he said,

"Lieutenant, mix up another mustard poultice, will you, and bring it here for Mrs. Ross? She's feeling poorly again."

Benjamin retrieved the flannel he'd left on the floor of the wagon. It was already stiff and cold but he gave it a few good snaps until most of the old paste fell out.

Grabbing the chipped moustache cup, he headed for the same family to ask for more hot water.

"I'm getting pretty good at this," he declared to himself as he set to work.

When the plaster was ready, he walked over and stood just outside the Ross tent.

"Here you go, Doc," he called loudly.

Dr. Powell reached out both hands to receive it.

"Thank you, Lieutenant. I won't be needing anything more tonight. See you in the morning."

"Yes, Sir, goodnight Sir," Benjamin said as he turned to leave.

On the way to the escorts' area, he stopped to remove Sonny's feedbag and water him again. Once he reached the officers' tent, he paused to look up at the bright crescent moon and the field of stars above him.

He thought about Hettie and wondered if she ever thought of him. Was the sky clear like this where she was and was she looking up at the moon right now like he was? Imagining that they were looking at the moon together made him feel close to her. For a moment, it felt almost real.

But, then, he found himself alone again, standing in the middle of the rows and rows of makeshift tents and shelters. He patted his inside vest pocket to check on his worn document case with the scrap of her dress pressed between its leaves.

He shuddered as a sudden chill started at his tailbone and ran upwards through his tired body. Shaking it off, he drew himself up and slowly filled his lungs one final time with the mingled sharp fragrances of the dying wood fires and the dank woods beyond.

Then he pulled open the canvas tent flap and reluctantly surrendered himself to the smell of the wet wool and unwashed bodies of his fellow officers that awaited him inside.

CHAPTER 20

LAME BEAR'S ORDEAL

Lame Bear's farm
Winter 1838–1839

Gabriel, sound asleep by the fireplace, was startled awake by Halfmoon's shouting. He sat up, blinking his eyes against the daylight, trying to get his bearings.

"That old lady hardly ever says two words to me and now there she is yelling her fool head off," he grumbled.

At first he couldn't figure out where she was. Grabbing his overalls from the floor beside him, he jumped to his feet and quickly pulled the pants up over his rumpled long underwear. He shrugged first one shoulder and then the other into the straps and then swayed his hips from side to side to free up his bunched up drawers while at the same time sinking his stocking feet into his cracked leather boots.

"Hold your horses," he shouted. "I'm coming, I'm coming."

When he stepped out the door, he spotted Halfmoon and Gertrude on the far side of the well, babbling and gesturing to each other. They were bent over a still gray form.

He began to run over to them, but the snow was too deep. Then he noticed the sisters' tracks and once he stepped over into them, the going was easier. As he got closer, he saw they were huddled over a body. A very still body.

"Who is it?" he called out.

"It's Lame Bear," Halfmoon answered, "and he's half froze to death. Hurry! Help us get him inside."

The three of them turned Lame Bear over, and then Gabriel moved around behind his head, reached down and got a firm grip under each armpit. As he started to lift the limp body out of the snow, he heard Lame Bear moan and then there was nothing. Walking backwards and bent almost double, Gabriel staggered towards the cabin dragging his heavy burden. All was quiet except for the squeaking of Lame Bear's leather leggings on the snow.

He felt a cold draft ruffle his hair as Halfmoon pushed past him, hurrying to get to the cabin first. Gertrude hovered alongside, darting here and there, getting in his way and tripping him as she tried to keep Lame Bear's flimsy gray blanket on top of his body.

Once inside, the women set right to work removing Lame Bear's stiff, wet clothing and wrapping him in the heavy Army-issue blankets Benjamin had left them for their own pallets. Then, with Gertrude kneeling near his head, and Halfmoon at his feet, they began to massage his ghostly pale hands and feet.

"He sure looks like a goner to me," Gabriel remarked to no one in particular as he stood over them, taking it all in.

Then he spotted Lame Bear's deformed feet. He'd heard he limped but he never expected anything like this. At first he couldn't make out any toes at all. The ends of his feet looked like knobby stumps. But then he found the toes. Pitifully twisted, they looked like they had been pressed by a flatiron and were bent back under the balls of his feet.

"Look at those feet, will you!" he exclaimed, leaning over to get a better look.

"How'd they get like that, anyhow?

"What happened to him? Are those really his toes? How'd he ever manage to walk on those things?

"And where's those others that was with him," he went on, "that girl Hettie, the one my brother's sweet on, and the grannie, and the deaf and dumb boy? Where they at?

"You don't think something happened to them, do you, and he came here for help?"

Halfmoon waited for him to wind down and then answered quietly,

"Lame Bear's feet have always been crooked. He was born that way."

She continued calmly, "Now, then, we can't let his hands and feet thaw out too quick. We'll be needing a pail of snow right off," she said reaching over for the rope handle on one of the water buckets and handing it up to him.

Soon the dirt floor was puddled with melting snow. The three of them took turns rubbing Lame Bear's frostbitten limbs, stoking the fire, bringing in fresh snow, and patiently spooning sips of Gertrude's warm, sweet broth into his mouth.

"You want me to go for help? Get my Maw?" Gabriel said to the sisters as the day wore on and Lame Bear remained unresponsive.

"I don't think there's anyone else left in these parts but I could be in Dalton by tonight and back here with my Maw or Paw by morning. Or maybe even find that barber in Dalton who works on people when they're sick or hurt."

Halfmoon rocked back on her heels and looked up at him.

"Wait," she said. "We'll wait 'til we see how he is after his hands and feet are warmed. There's nothing more to be done until then, anyhow."

She continued to speak, but so quietly Gabriel almost couldn't hear her.

"Time was, before the killing sicknesses came, my husband, Kookowee, was *shaman* for our village. He healed many, many people, even some stricken with the pox."

Gertrude nodded in agreement.

"But, in the end, hard as he tried, when our own children took sick with the pox, he couldn't save them, and after the three of them passed on, one after the other, if he didn't come down with it too. Sickened and died in less than two days time, he did.

"Still, I learned much healing from him and this is how he'd do."

For once, Gabriel was almost at a loss for words.

"Kookowee?" he finally blurted out. "Kookowee was your husband? Why, I've heard of him. He's famous in our parts."

Then he stopped and rolled his eyes.

"I'm sorry Miss Halfmoon. I didn't mean no disrespect about the barber and all. I'm just wanting to help."

"It's alright, Gabriel," she said, "I understand."

He couldn't keep still for long, though.

"Say, how's about I follow Lame Bear's tracks back the way he came? Maybe I can find out what happened to the others. How about it?"

"No, Gabriel," she said, "Stay here with us. That's what your brother would want, and, besides, it's much too dangerous to set out on your own in all this cold.

"Now, then, go and help Gertrude bring in the wood. Can't you see she needs help? And after that, fetch two, three buckets of water, and, while you're at it, some more snow too. One more batch will just about do it."

"Yes, Ma'am. Right away, Ma'am," Gabriel said as he scrambled to catch up with Gertrude who was waiting at the door and smiling shyly at him.

The Cave

The twins were acquiring new survival skills all the time, but there was such an unrelieved sameness to their lives that they were not often aware of it. They longed for the old life.

CHAPTER 21

THE ROAD NOT TAKEN

The Trail of Tears
Early January 1839

Unfortunately, Quatie Ross was not getting better. The doses of calomel and laudanum, which Dr. Powell administered each evening, were having less and less effect. He would often call on Ben for a plaster to help her through the night but even that didn't seem to be doing much good anymore.

One evening, drawing Ben away from young Silas and George, the worried doctor said in a low voice, "She seems even more short of breath tonight and her heart is weak.

"She tries not to let on, but it's clear to me that she's in a lot of pain," he told Benjamin.

"That jolting she's taking in her carriage every day is taking its toll, and I wouldn't be surprised if she hasn't cracked some ribs. I don't know how much more she can stand."

So far, in spite of much sickness, their group had suffered no deaths even though some of the other removal parties were reporting them almost daily. Ben was afraid that Quatie Ross, so gentle and caring, would be their first.

He tried to remember some of the homemade remedies his grandmother and mother used for bronchitis and influenza and he also took special note of the infusions and potions the Cherokees mixed up to treat themselves but, so far, he hadn't been able to come up with anything new to suggest to Dr. Powell.

On the other hand, Jesse Birdsong, Benjamin's first patient, was getting stronger every day. He was back walking the trail with his family and even helping to pull their heavy cartload of belongings. Whenever they passed each other on the trail, Birdie would give his chest an exaggerated thump, Ben would give his own a thump in return, and they would share a hearty laugh. The ritual was a bright spot in an otherwise dismal day and Ben always looked forward to it.

On their twenty-first night on the trail, just off the Nashville Road and still a day's march away from Paducah, Quatie's worsening health reached the breaking point. Word quickly spread throughout the camp. A small group of concerned Cherokees gathered outside the Ross's tent waiting for word of her condition.

After examining and treating her, Dr. Powell, with Benjamin at his side, finished the rest of his evening rounds before returning to apply a mustard plaster.

As they approached the tent, they spotted Chief Ross, only just back from an overnight trip to confer with Thomas Clark, one of his contractors.

"Mr. Ross, Sir," Dr. Powell called out, "May I have a word with you?"

"Of course, Dr. Powell. How are you and Lieutenant Stone this evening?" Ross said, greeting them.

Dr. Powell stepped forward and began to speak.

"Sir, I am sorry to have to inform you that, in my professional opinion, your wife's condition is very grave. Each day the congestion in her lungs grows worse and she was not in good health to begin with. Also, she appears to be in a great deal of pain, especially when she coughs. And, now, your daughter, Miss Jane, reports that today she has taken almost no nourishment.

"You must realize, Sir, that her heart is not strong, and she cannot continue much longer in this weakened state. Frankly, I fear that her demise is just a matter of time, perhaps only a few days hence, unless she is given a respite from this terrible journey."

Chief Ross sighed and rubbed his hand across his forehead.

"I know that what you are telling me is true, Doctor, and I thank you for your candor and for all the care you are giving my dear wife. I've known for some time that she was getting worse, and I am relieved to tell you that, even as we speak, arrangements are being made for our transfer to a water route for the remainder of the journey.

"We had hoped to travel all the way on these trails with our people in order to help them in this time of great need and sorrow but I know it is no longer possible.

"We have been able to secure a boat which will be waiting for us when we reach Paducah. It is a small paddle wheel towboat called the *Victoria,* able to accommodate not only my family but also others from our group who are in need of special assistance. The boat already holds Conductor John Drew's small removal party and is late arriving because it was delayed by low water in the Tennessee River but it has certainly come at an extremely opportune time for my wife.

"Those who can't be accommodated on the boat will proceed as before," he said. "Mr. Dudley, the wagon master, is even now drawing up the lists."

Dr. Powell said, "Sir, what you're saying is good news, and almost certainly will help your wife."

Ross nodded and then turned to Benjamin.

"Lieutenant, Mr. Dudley will be speaking with you later this evening about accompanying us on the *Victoria.* Dr. Powell is needed here but we feel confident that the medical care you can provide will be most helpful to my wife and the others on this voyage."

Benjamin was stunned.

"Excuse me for saying so, Sir," he blurted out, "but I haven't got any medical training at all. None. What little I do know I've only picked up here on the trail, watching Dr. Powell.

"I'm sorry, Sir, but I'm sure I'm not the one you want. I need the Doc, here, right beside me. I don't know enough to do any doctoring on my own."

"I understand your concerns, Lieutenant," Chief Ross said, "but Dr. Powell cannot be spared and as his assistant you are the most qualified to serve in his place. We need you. My wife needs you."

"Yes, Sir." Benjamin said numbly.

Chief Ross and Dr. Powell entered the tent to attend to Quatie, and Benjamin was left to stand by himself. He glanced over at Sonny who was grazing in back of the tents, patiently pulling shriveled stubs of brown grass out of the thin covering of brittle ice.

Ben knew he shouldn't be worrying about a horse when people's lives were at stake, but he couldn't help it. He knew there'd be no room for Sonny on the *Victoria.*

The handsome gelding raised his head and snorted softly as Benjamin approached and laid his chapped unshaven cheek against the warm shaggy fur. Sonny turned his head slightly, cocking one tufted ear.

Then he began to playfully toss his head up and down.

"Whoa, Boy," Ben said softly. "Whoa there."

He reached out and combed his fingers through the stiff strands of Sonny's mane. He remembered his first day as a green recruit when Sonny was assigned to him. He couldn't believe this powerful, good-looking animal was being turned over to him. The two of them quickly became an inseparable team, settling into a comfortable routine as they shared and successfully completed one task after another.

"Oh, Sonny, I can't stand to lose you now. What's to become of you? With me gone, who's to look after you?"

Benjamin felt a hand on his shoulder.

Dr. Powell had followed him over and now spoke quietly.

"I know how you feel about that horse, Son. I feel the same way about my old bay. I'll see that he's taken care of for you. In fact, I'll speak to Mr. Dudley tonight. After all you've done to help me, it's the least I can do.

"And when we reach Indian Territory, I'll make arrangements for him to be stabled with the cavalry at Fort Gibson until you can pick him up. You have my word."

Ben, with a relieved smile on his face, reached out to shake his hand.

"Thank you, Sir, thank you so much. I really appreciate it. He means the world to me, that's for sure."

CHAPTER 22

THE BLACK ROT

Lame Bear's farm
Early January 1839

"Who's the white boy?" Lame Bear whispered to Halfmoon.

"Gertrude!" she called, "Come here. Finally, after almost two weeks, Lame Bear's awake."

"Who's the boy?" he asked again. "Where'd he come from?"

"Name's Gabriel Stone. He's the brother of Benjamin Stone. Remember him?" Halfmoon said as Gertrude, who'd been adding wood to the fire, hurried over.

"Lame Bear," Halfmoon said. "Tell us where are Mattie Poor and the twins? Are they safe?"

When she saw that he was too weak to speak again so quickly, she continued on to give him more time.

"Benjamin Stone, he's one of those Georgia soldiers who did that last batch of surveying and came that time and took your rifle. Ours too. Remember? Well then he switched from the Guard over to General Scott's Army, and he and some of the others came back last spring, in May, it was, and took us prisoner: Gertrude and me, the Pritchards too. Isn't that right, Gertrude?

"Kept us fenced up in those dirty, nasty places. First in New Echota and then in Rattlesnake Springs, right through the hot summer and the harvest season and even on into the winter too. It was a bad time. There was much sickness in those terrible places and many of us died."

Halfmoon bit her lip at the painful memories that flooded back over her and looked down at Lame Bear again. She could see that he was listening intently but, from time to time, the effort was causing him to sigh deeply.

"But, you know something?" she said softly. "If it wasn't for Benjamin Stone, Gertrude and me, why we'd be marching west on that trail of death ourselves, that's for sure.

"After he put us in that stockade, almost right off, seems he had a change of heart. Fact is, from then on, he tried to help us through all those hard times, even brought us food most days.

"And, would you believe it, the night before the Army was getting ready to move us out, he borrowed a mule and wagon from his folks in Dalton and came back with his brother Gabriel, here, to get us. He walked into that depot, bold as you please, and snatched us right out from under their noses. Had Gabriel bring us on up here in the wagon.

"Right now, he's on his way west himself. The Army put him on as a guard, escort they call it, for the last party heading out, the John Ross Party. We'd be in that one ourselves if it weren't for him.

"This here place belongs to him now. He went and bought it back from the Campbells, those squatters who stole it from you in the land lottery. He's even given us the papers to prove it," she continued as Gertrude nodded in agreement.

"Says it's for you and your family, but he really did it for Hester. Says he plans to come back soon as he can to get her, if she'll have him that is. Says he loves her.

"But that's enough for now. Lame Bear. Try to tell us about Mattie Poor and the twins? Are they all right? Where are they?"

Lame Bear raised himself up on one elbow and glanced uneasily over at Gabriel.

"Gabriel's a good boy, Lame Bear," Halfmoon said. "You can trust him."

Lame Bear took a deep breath. "They're hiding out near Turtle Rock. You remember that deep cave cut high up, not far from the waterfall and the Rock? Kookowee and I used to sleep there once in a while when we were out hunting. Remember?

"It's cold and wet up there and they're mighty hungry besides, but they're safe. I left them because I'd become a burden. Just one more person for them to take care of.

"But now it looks like all I've done is put more on your shoulders, instead," he said, looking around, and then closing his eyes.

"No, Lame Bear, you're not a burden," Halfmoon said firmly.

"Gertrude and me, we're thankful you came here. This is your mother's home and it's where you and your family belong."

"We got away to the cave the same day the soldiers took you," Lame Bear said. "Mattie sent Hester and Sky to your place that morning and from the hilltop just past Moogan's, they saw the soldiers arresting you. They ran all the way back to warn us so we could get away. Are they still looking for us, do you know?"

"No, no more," Halfmoon answered. "Far as we can tell, nobody's in danger anymore. They got what they wanted—our homes—our land—everything—except for those farms over near Quallatown, which they can't touch because of Will Thomas.

"I'm afraid most all our people are gone west by now. I don't think there's anyone left around Ellijay or New Echota anymore unless they're hiding somewhere up in the hills like you. All that's left of our Nation, outside of Quallatown, in these parts anyway, is just this one place, and even that belongs to the white man now."

Lame Bear sighed and closed his eyes again as he listened to Halfmoon. The dull but steady pain throughout his body took over, and he became aware for the first time of the awful heaviness of his hands. It took great effort to lift them. Opening his eyes, he gravely inspected the two masses of swollen yellow and purple pulp.

He stared in fascination at the shredded iridescent blisters undulating on the backs of his hands. Then he gasped in horror as he realized that it wasn't his own waxy skin that was quivering. It was several creamy-white maggots cleaning out the decaying flesh on each of his hands.

"Your hands are healing, Lame Bear," Halfmoon reassured him as she gently took his arms and lowered them back down onto the soft nests Gertrude had made on either side of his pallet.

"They're not as bad as they look. The worms have done their job well. Why already there's healthy new skin growing underneath.

"Your feet, though, that's another matter."

Taken aback, Lame Bear tried to lift himself up to look but the effort was too great.

"Your feet are the worst," she said as matter-of-factly as she could.

"Most of your toes, they've been dropping off, one by one. But they weren't any good to you anyhow, now were they?" she said, not unkindly. "Maybe now, without them, you'll be able to walk easier.

"But, today, if that isn't bad enough, we've found something more. When Gertrude was tending to you this morning, she noticed two little spots of black rot on one of your feet.

"Right now, it doesn't look too bad but you know as well as we do those spots will fester and spread until your whole leg turns green and rots away if we don't attend to them right away.

"And, you know something? If we don't cut it all out, before long, that *Raven Mocker of Death* will be sitting in the tree outside the door calling for you.

"You know what has to be done, don't you Lame Bear?" she asked. "I'll do my best to get it all the first time.

"You understand, Lame Bear?" she asked again. "There's no other way. It has to be done and right quick."

"Yes," he answered, closing his eyes. "I understand."

"I'm sorry, but there's no way round it," she said again, standing up and backing away.

"Here now, will you look at that. Gertrude's gone and got some of her broth all warmed up and ready for you. She'll help you with that and then you must try to rest, as best you can, until it's time to begin."

She wrapped herself in her shawl and went out to find Gabriel who'd stepped outside. They would need him to help hold Lame Bear.

Meanwhile, Gertrude, with the bowl of steaming broth balanced in her hands, slowly knelt down and took her place at his side. She dipped one knuckle cautiously into the bowl and, satisfied that it wasn't too hot, licked her finger clean and fished the spoon out of her apron pocket.

Starting at the edge of the broth, she slowly pressed the bowl of the spoon into the thick, rich mixture and allowed it to fill. Holding it up, she blew gently across the surface, and carefully trickled the contents into Lame Bear's half open mouth and onto his waiting tongue. Each time he swallowed she rewarded him with soft little clucking noises.

At the end, their eyes met for just an instant, and a silent understanding of the need for strength and courage passed between them.

CHAPTER 23

THE *VICTORIA*

The Trail of Tears
Southeast of Paducah, Kentucky
January 1839

The following morning Wagon Master Dudley read aloud the lists that divided the party. When all the teams were hitched up and the wagons and carts loaded, Quatie was gently carried out and propped up in her carriage. Her face was stained with tears, and looked pinched and stark against the quilted black leather upholstery. She spoke slowly, haltingly, to the Cherokees gathered around her who strained to catch her soft words.

"My friends—forgive me for being such a burden—I'm so sorry—I know I'll be back on my feet again in no time at all."

She took a deep rattling breath. "But now, they tell me I have to leave you—you must go on without me—be strong, even though I am not—goodbye my dear, dear comrades—God Speed."

Then, with the Ross carriage leading the way, the smaller band of Cherokees wended its way out of the campground towards the port at Paducah. Ben, his knapsack on his back, assumed his usual place at the end of the line. This time, however, he was on foot.

After a long day's march, they reached the outskirts of Paducah just as the sun was setting. When they proceeded down the main street to the river, Ben was surprised to see that the *Victoria* seemed very small and plain compared to the other steamboats moored there. Except for her tall, shiny black stacks with their crimped tops, he didn't see anything special about this little boat.

He helped carry Mrs. Ross on board and waited outside her door until she was settled in the little cabin she would be sharing with her daughter Jane. Then he dosed her with the calomel and laudanum that Dr. Powell had prescribed.

"No plaster please," she said. "Not tonight. Good night Lieutenant and thank you."

"Yes, Ma'am. Goodnight Ma'am. Goodnight Miss Jane," he said, shutting the cabin door behind him.

Ben had been assigned to a hammock in the crew's quarters below but before heading there, he wanted to read his new orders once more and decided to take advantage of the bright light provided by a giant fire pot mounted on the railing just outside Quatie's cabin.

The *Victoria,* with its Cherokee detachment under the command of Conductor John Drew, was to take them from Paducah down the Ohio River, and westward onto the Mississippi, which some Cherokees called the Great Father River. But Ben knew that others called it *Uktena,* the serpent of the underworld, because they said it was more like an evil snake than a father, winding and squeezing in on itself with many treacherous shoals and underwater snags waiting to tear unsuspecting boats to pieces.

"And being winter just adds to those dangers," he thought.

They would follow the Mississippi south, his orders stated, until they reached a place called Montgomery's Point. There, they would find another mighty river, the Arkansas, which would take them farther west.

They would disembark at Little Rock in Arkansas, he read, and travel overland to Fort Smith where they'd pick up provisions at the Fort's Commissary located near Camp Belknap and then move on about forty miles more to Fort Gibson, their final destination on the Indian Reservation itself.

Nearby, he heard someone noisily clearing his throat, and when he looked up, he discovered Mr. Bingham, the gap-toothed first mate, waiting impatiently to take him below. As Bingham lead the way, it was obvious that the old man wasn't about to wait around for Ben to get used to the ship's ladders.

"Move along, now. You're making me late for me dinner," he grumped. "You clumsy soldiers, you're all alike. Thanks to you, there's probably no bread left on the line and no meat in the stew. I ain't got all day. So, hurry up, will ya!"

In the mess, Ben felt curious eyes on him as he eagerly ate everything on his plate. It was the best food he'd eaten since his last night home. He polished it all off, including every last sliver of bread and blob of grease before rising to follow Mr. Bingham again.

They reached the hammocks fitted along the sides of the keel in the belly of the boat. Some were already lumpy with occupants.

Mr. Bingham gestured, "This one's yourn, but, mind you, they take some getting used to."

After studying it for a moment, Benjamin spread open the hammock with both hands and tentatively placed one knee directly into the center of the netting. It wobbled at first but with most of his weight on the other leg, he felt pretty steady. So far so good.

He looked up to see that he and Bingham had company. Two firemen had taken a break from wooding to watch the action. He sensed that this was not going to be as easy as it looked.

Very carefully, he leaned over and inched his upper body towards his now firmly planted knee while slowly disengaging his pivot foot. And just as slowly, the hammock rolled him over and cast him out onto the planking like so much jetsam.

Loud laughter followed. It woke the man in the next hammock who lifted his head to see what was going on.

"I can do this," Ben muttered as he dusted himself off and stepped forward again. This time, after spreading the hammock's sides, he rotated his body around and cautiously centered his backside directly over the abyss, took a deep breath, and plopped himself down. Before it could spew him out again, he threw his upper body into the fray and quickly heaved his legs up and over the side.

The hammock swung violently back and forth as he clutched at the webbing. Finally, it reluctantly accepted his presence and settled down to a gentle swaying.

"Your boots, boy, you forgot your boots," Mr. Bingham hooted, slapping his thighs.

"Damn the boots, Sir," Ben sputtered over his shoulder. I'm in this thing now!"

"Well, enjoy it while you can, lad, 'cause tomorrow night Captain says you'll be taking your turn standing watch just like the rest of us."

Ben laid his tired head onto the hard canvas pad sewn into the netting to serve as a pillow, and tried to get comfortable. Squashed elbow to elbow with burly strangers, he wondered if he would ever get used to sleeping all trussed up like a turkey.

Already queasy from the rocking of the boat, he longed for Hettie and the hills of Georgia. As he lay there waiting for sleep, he wondered if he'd ever see her again and how much more he would have to endure before he could get back home to Georgia.

But the next morning, even though the air was cold with a stiff breeze, the sun was shining. After a breakfast of hominy grits and chicory coffee, he checked on the Ross family, and then decided to go out on deck and find a sunny spot out of the wind.

He settled himself down, propping his back against the rough boards of the wheelhouse to take in the ever-changing scenery. He was prepared for the endless woods and farmland but the many settlements and pockets of commerce along the river were unexpected. And after the red clay of Georgia, he was surprised at the rich black earth of the farms along the shores.

He let his mind reflect back to his mother and father and then on to Gabriel. He wondered how he was faring with the old sisters on Lame Bear's, now his, farm.

Had Hettie been found and, if so, did she know what he was trying to do to make amends? Did she care? And if she had already come down out of the hills, would she still be around when he got back home? What if she found someone else in the meantime? Gabriel, for instance.

"Young as he is, that boy's as handsome as they come and mighty grown for his age, too. But he knows how I feel about her and I do believe he'll respect that."

He'd seen, though, that day in the field above Lame Bear's place, that Venable Guinnett had his eye on her too. Even before he'd realized how he felt about her himself. But the last he'd heard, Venable and the removal party he was escorting were trapped on the Kentucky side of the Mississippi across from Cape Girardeau in Missouri. They said the ice from upriver kept breaking off and sending massive frozen chunks, some as big as houses, barreling downstream so that half the Cherokees in the party couldn't ferry across.

He'd heard the situation was desperate, with more and more Cherokees freezing to death every day. The suffering must be terrible, he thought, but he also realized that at least for now, Venable was no threat to him.

While he was daydreaming, he absently picked up a square chunk of pine from the wood stacked next to him and after turning it over in his hand several times, took out the folding pocket knife his father had given him on his twelfth birthday, and idly began to pare off strips of bark.

After a while, he became aware that he was being watched. Four or five Cherokee children, including Silas and George Ross, were gathering round.

"This could be a little bird, don't you think?" he asked, holding up the piece of wood.

Nobody said a word.

He spoke again. "Does this look anything like a bird to you?

"Let's see what we can do. Shall I make it into a little wren?" he asked a small girl peeking out from behind the boys.

He recognized her sad little face. Her father was very ill. Dr. Powell said it was consumption and recommended the water route for the pair.

"How about a Carolina wren?" he suggested, looking at her.

Embarrassed at the attention, she backed off, but as he began to chip away, he noticed her inching forward again.

Before long he had produced an egg shaped lump. He held it up for inspection.

"Where's the head and tail on this thing? Anybody know?" He said, pretending to study it.

"How about this end for the tail," he said pointing to one end.

"What about it?"

Hearing no answer, he shrugged and went back to carving until he had the beginnings of the body of a plump little bird with a sensible tail. By now most of the little ones were nestled comfortably around him, jostling each other to catch and finger the shavings as they dropped off. Even the little girl—he thought her name was Tuti—kept creeping closer.

When he decided the body and tail were about as good as he could do, he took his knife and carved out long curving lines for the feathers.

"The head and beak, now, they're going to be a lot harder," he explained in a very serious voice to the children.

"It's been a while since I've done any carving at all and, to tell you the God's honest truth, I never was much good at it to begin with. In fact, if you must know, I was about the worst one of all the bigger boys in my school."

But he stuck with it and eventually produced a rough-hewn head and bill to go with the rest of his bird.

"Now for the finishing touches," he announced grandly, blowing off the sawdust.

Using the point of his blade, he spiraled deep into the wood until he had incised a little circle on each side of the head for the eyes. Then, with quick choppy strokes, he whittled away until he'd formed the characteristic little upturned beak of a Carolina wren. Frankly amazed at the outcome, he held it up for the children to see.

"Well, that about does it," he said proudly.

Looking around, he spotted the little girl.

"Here, Tuti. That is your name isn't it? This one's yours," he said.

Smiling, he leaned over and held it out to her.

"Here you go."

Startled, she shrank back from him. When he stood up to try to hand it to her, she darted away altogether amidst much laughter and teasing from the boys.

An adult voice surprised him.

"I'll see that she gets it, Lieutenant," Mrs. Ross said, holding onto the doorway of her cabin.

"Thank you for thinking of her," she added.

"Yes, Ma'am," Ben said, handing the toy to her.

"May I be of any assistance to you at this time?"

"No thank you, not at the present. Later, perhaps," she said, as she stepped back inside. He could hear her croup-like coughing even through the closed cabin door.

Later that night, after he'd listened to her lungs and dosed her with calomel and laudanum, he mixed a mustard plaster for her and gave it to Jane to administer. Then he went below to see to the medical needs of the other passengers and crew.

He found a small cluster of ailing Cherokees along with one crewman with an angry red carbuncle on his cheek. Mr. Bingham had them all lined up, and was standing by, puffed up with his own importance, waiting to be of assistance.

"Why didn't I pay more attention to the doc and my grandmother when I had the chance?" Ben reproached himself as he set up his medical supplies and got out the stethoscope and the brass case of lancets he had borrowed from Dr. Powell.

"If these people only knew what's good for them," he thought, "they'd keep their boils and other ailments to themselves."

"I'll do the best I can for them," he vowed, "but it'll be a miracle if I don't kill somebody before this whole thing's over. And that's a fact."

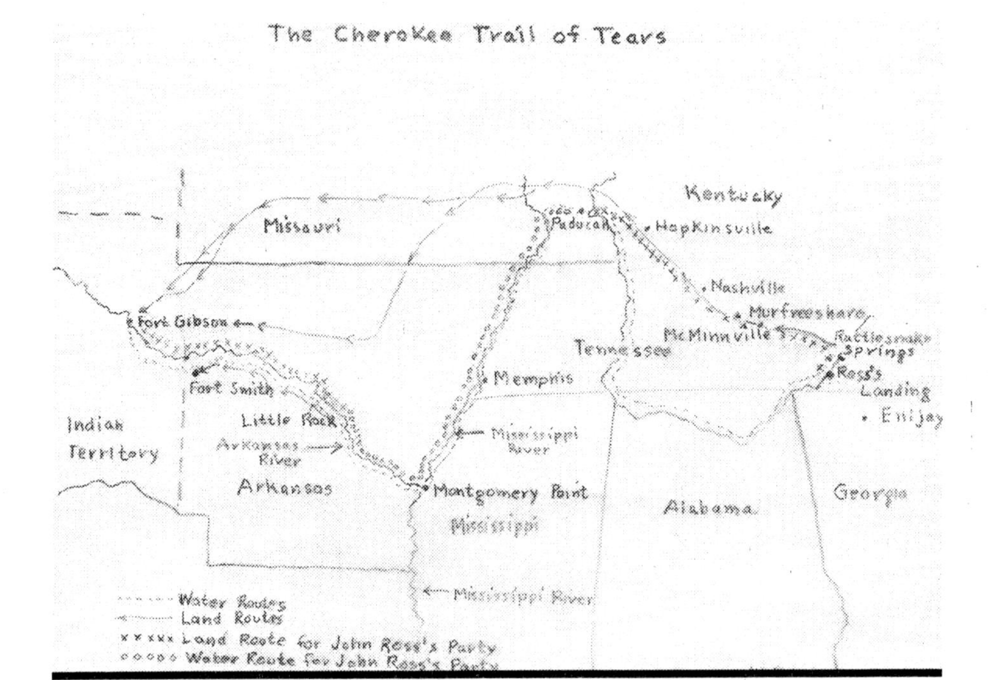

Map of The Trail of Tears 1838–1839

CHAPTER 24

IS IT SAFE TO COME HOME?

The Great Smoky Mountains
Late January 1839

Gabriel, leading Sadie along by her halter, was keyed up as he made his way up into the mountains to bring Lame Bear's family home. At long last, he was going to get to see what was so wonderful about this family. He was especially curious about Hettie.

"What makes her so different from all those good looking girls around Dalton that Ben never paid no mind to?" he thought. "What's so special about this one, anyhow?"

He could hear Halfmoon huffing and puffing as she struggled along behind him. He kept slowing down for her even though he was eager to get to Turtle Rock. She was taking forever and he wished he could have come by himself. He would have, a long time ago, if it had been up to him. But Halfmoon wouldn't let him. She kept saying she'd be ready as soon as they were sure the black rot on Lame Bear's foot was gone for good.

Now he was just hoping she'd be able to make it all the way. Her hair, usually piled neatly on top of her head and pinned up with a tortoise shell comb, had come undone and long strands of it were clinging to her face.

"You want to ride on the mule, Ma'am?" he finally asked, peering around Sadie's middle at the determined old lady behind him.

"It's pretty rocky through here. You might just as well be riding."

"No, thank you," Halfmoon said firmly, stopping to catch her breath.

"That would be too hard on your mule, and, besides, we need to save her for later. Who knows what we'll find once we get up there," she said as she fumbled with her comb and tried to redo her hair with her fingers.

"For all we know, Mattie Poor may be too weak to walk and we want to get the three of them back home before dark."

She caught his eye. "Unless, of course, you feel like spending the night up there in that old cave."

"No Ma'am. Not me," Gabriel protested, laughing at the thought of it. "Not me!"

She waved her walking stick at him. "Now then, let's get going. Hurry up. We've rested long enough. And, don't forget, when we get close, I want you to stay with the mule while I go on by myself. If Mattie Poor sees you, she'll think you're here to take them in.

"Something tells me we're getting right close now," she continued. "Keep a sharp lookout for that rock, you hear me?"

"Yes, Ma'am," he answered, clucking at Sadie.

They had started out just before sunrise with the saddlebags bulging with food. Gertrude had been baking double for the past two days, ever since Halfmoon had decided it was safe to leave Lame Bear.

He seemed stronger every day. The whites of his eyes were still as yellow as saffron but the raccoon circles were fading and his breathing seemed easier too. And over the past few days, whenever he needed something, he'd started dragging himself around the cabin on his buttocks, with the tender stumps of his feet held safely out of the way. He was coughing less, too. The time was definitely right to fetch Mattie Poor and the twins.

Lame Bear was determined to go with them. He thought he should be the one to bring his own family home.

"I'll ride on the back of that mule of Gabriel's. She can carry me," he announced.

Hands on hips, Halfmoon fixed him with a stare.

"A lot of help you'd be," she finally said. "What do you think will happen to your feet if we get caught in the rain or Sadie stumbles? You ready for more cutting and scraping? I'm not, and that's a fact."

She sighed and her tone softened. "But you know something Lame Bear? Gabriel and me, we'll do just fine by ourselves, and we'll be back home with the rest of them before you know it."

And so the old woman, the young boy, and the little mule had set out just after sunrise to bring home the rest of the family.

As he trudged along, Gabriel kept a sharp eye out for Turtle Rock. Finally after they had followed another long bend in the river, they began to hear the sound of a waterfall and before long they spied Turtle Rock. It was still covered with snowdrifts but, even so, there was no mistaking its shape.

"I'll be leaving you now," Halfmoon said. "Stay close by and wait for my signal."

"Yes Ma'am, I will," he promised.

"Pay attention now and stay right here," she warned again as she started off without him.

She soon disappeared from view and, before long he began to hear her as she called out over and over in a high singsong voice to her old friend.

"Yoo hoo, Mattie Poor, yoo hoo, it's me! Come to take you home. Yoo hoo, Mattie Poor, yoo hoo, it's me, Halfmoon, come to take you home."

Gabriel hitched Sadie to a tree and sat down on a rock. After a while Halfmoon's voice grew faint until, at last, he could hear it only in his head.

It was at that moment, when all was quiet around him that he began to sense something wasn't quite right. He didn't know what it was. He thought he'd heard a slight noise in the brush up ahead but after listening carefully he couldn't be sure. And then he heard it again.

"There it is again," he whispered, sure now. He could hear a faint but unmistakable rustling in the underbrush off to his left. It seemed to be closing in, then stopping, and starting again.

"That's no animal," he breathed. It made his skin crawl, and he began to glance uneasily around him. Cautiously he got to his feet.

Sadie stopped grazing, lifted her head, and pricked up her ears. He shuddered and slowly backed up until he was braced defensively against the curve of her warm flank.

For sure, he knew he wasn't alone anymore. And he knew with certainty that those were human eyes he felt boring into him. Someone was out there, all right, tracking his every move. Warily, he crouched down and began to slowly bob and weave, trying to prepare himself for a surprise attack.

Out of the corner of his eye, he detected movement in a stand of tall trees to his left, just beyond an open grassy area. A boy his own age, tall and gaunt, emerged and began to walk towards him with his arms stretched out in front of him, the palms of his hands turned upwards.

Gabriel straightened up and gasped with relief as he realized who it must be.

"Why, you're the deaf and dumb boy! You're Hettie's brother," he cried out.

Gabriel was shocked to see how thin the boy was in his ragged clothing. He took a step forward and assumed the same peace gesture by holding his hands straight out with his palms facing up.

When Sky reached him, they touched hands, and smiled at each other. Gabriel turned slightly and took a step backwards as he reached into one of the saddlebags. He pulled out a loaf of Gertrude's bread and held it out in friendship to the hollow-eyed man-child.

"Sky! That's your name. Say, I remember now! Here, Sky, have some bread." Touching his own chest he said, "My name's Gabriel."

Sky took the loaf of bread, bit off a large chunk and stuffed it into his mouth, almost choking as he wolfed it down. But after another mouthful, he stopped suddenly, grunting softly as he pulled off a fistful and held it out to Gabriel.

Together the two boys savored Gertrude's offering, all the while sizing each other up. Gabriel was just in the process of offering Sky a drink of water from his canteen when he heard the disgusted voice of Halfmoon as she came bustling around the bend.

"Why didn't you answer my signal, Boy?" she scolded. "Would you believe it? I found Mattie Poor and Hester right off, but Sky wasn't there. He's out hunting somewhere. But all three, they're safe and sound, and right now Mattie Poor and Hester are gathering their things together so they can leave the cave soon as Sky gets back.

"Didn't you hear me calling for you to come? I told you to pay attention! What's the matter with you? We need to get right back up there with the mule to help them pack up."

Then she spotted Sky standing on the other side of the mule.

"Oh, my Lord, you've found Sky...Sky, Sky," she cried.

Sky rushed to her with his arms outstretched.

With new tears rolling down her already wet cheeks, she clasped him tightly to her. He bent his knees so that his head would fit into the softness of her shoulder.

Crooning softly to him, she kept hugging and hugging him, pulling back from him once or twice so that she could look in his face, and then hugging him some more.

"Sky," she finally said, tapping him lightly on the shoulder and pointing to Gabriel.

"This here's Gabriel who helped save Gertrude and me, and now he's here with me to bring you home."

Then, smiling in spite of her tears, she reached for Gabriel's arm and pulled him into their embrace.

Gabriel had never felt so silly in all his life but he didn't try to pull away. It felt too good.

Chapter 25

Quatie

The Arkansas River
Near Little Rock, Arkansas
Late January 1839

Within the next few days, the *Victoria* was expected to dock at the port of Little Rock. The last part of the trip to Indian Territory would be made over land. After days and days of sleet, icy winds, rough water, and the constant threat of collisions with hidden shoals and deadly ice floes, Ben was more than ready for dry land.

The good news was that Quatie Ross seemed to be holding her own and Ben was hopeful that she could withstand the last part of the trip in a wagon. He heard that the roads and trails in Arkansas were in better shape than those in Tennessee and Kentucky, and, besides, Quatie was getting stronger every day. Everyone noticed it. He was especially encouraged by the bright rosy glow that began to appear on her otherwise pale cheeks, especially in the late afternoons.

Most mornings, even on the worst days, she appeared outside her cabin to take a daily constitutional. Wrapped in her heavy cloak with the hood pulled tightly around her face, she would cling precariously to the railing, and with great effort, pull herself along, hand over hand, with Miss Jane and Ben hovering protectively alongside. As she worked her way down the covered passageway, she would stop frequently to greet fellow passengers and crew members, asking after their health and that of their loved ones. She knew everybody's name.

When she reached the bow, she would settle herself on the leeward side of the upper deck on one of the long backless spectator benches. It seemed to Ben that some of her happiest times occurred when the boat was docked for wooding. Even on the coldest days, she liked to watch the firemen as they moved back and forth loading the wood for the giant boilers. If it were a calm, windless day, she would untie the drawstring of her hood, uncover her head, and raise her face to the warmth of the sun.

Little Tuti, with her solemn dark eyes and straight black hair cut into bangs, was very fond of Mrs. Ross and often came to share the bench with her. The two seemed to have a special bond. Tuti would usually be carrying her little carved bird, and Quatie would begin the conversation by asking after it. As they sat and watched the activity below, they would chat like old friends.

When the wooding was completed, the captain would give a series of double toned blasts on the boat's whistle, and Quatie would stand up to make her way back to her cabin while the footing was still good. At her door, she'd straighten up, take a deep breath, and graciously bid everyone good morning before turning and stepping delicately over the high threshold into the dark cabin.

Along with all the Cherokees on board, Ben thought the world of her. Like Hettie, she was always on his mind, and he wanted so much to help her. She never complained about taking the daily doses of laudanum and calomel that Dr. Powell had prescribed, but she didn't like the evening mustard plasters, and, unless her breathing was especially labored, she politely but firmly refused them. She insisted that her ribs felt much better anyway although Ben could see it still hurt her to cough.

Lately, he'd been thinking about trying an old homemade remedy handed down in his family for generations that he hoped might help her. They called it Mother's Comfort and both his grandmother and his mother swore by it. They claimed it was good for everything from consumption to counteracting the effects of miasma.

He wasn't sure how he was going to mix it up to use on board the *Victoria,* however, because the captain had given orders that no alcohol was to be dispensed to the Indians without his permission. Also he didn't know how Quatie herself would feel about taking an elixir with spirits in it.

Still he felt that Mother's Comfort might be just what she needed. The old standby certainly had gotten his family through some terrible times. Like the time he'd come close to drowning.

During the winter of his last year at the one room schoolhouse in Dalton, he, with Gabriel in tow, had decided to take a shortcut home over the ice on the pond. Gabriel was only nine years old, but Ben, at fourteen, should have known better.

When they got halfway across the pond, the ice had begun to groan and then crack and splinter. Just before Ben lost his balance and fell backward into the fault, he managed to shove Gabriel to safety, shouting,

"Run! Get help! Go!"

Shocked into breathlessness and treading water furiously, he tried over and over to thrust his body up and out of the water. Each time however, the ice broke off in jagged shards, which slashed at his hands and arms as he sank back into the frigid water.

Finally, on the seventh try, he managed to anchor both elbows over the edge of the rippled surface and then wiggle and squirm his way out of the water. Lying flat and sobbing and shaking uncontrollably, he used his elbows to drag his heavy, sodden body across the surface of the ice, not daring to get up on his hands and knees until he was almost to the shore and safety.

Numbed to the bone and bleeding heavily, he lurched his way towards home. When he saw Gabriel leading his parents back over the fields towards him, he expected the worst, but to his surprise, they were not angry with him, although his mother, with tears in her eyes, had reproached him for putting both boys in such danger.

While he was warming up and getting his wounds attended to, his grandmother stirred together and heated his first dose of Mother's Comfort. He remembered the shock and surprise of the hot bitter taste and the terrible stinging in his throat as he swallowed. But he also remembered the incredible warmth that soon engulfed him from somewhere deep inside. At the same time, the taste of the honey in the mixture stayed behind to soothe away the burning in his throat. He could still bring back the sweet cloying sensation of that syrup on his tongue and how warm, loved, and deliciously drowsy it had made him feel.

He wanted the same for Quatie. He felt fairly sure the captain would give him the whiskey for medicinal purposes but, after making inquiries with the cook and among the crew, he could not find a drop of honey anywhere on board. He needed dried lemon peel, too. But luxuries like that were simply not available on a sparsely fitted, overcrowded boat like the *Victoria.*

"If worst comes to worst," he said, "I guess I can use sugar, but, come to think of it, I haven't seen any of that around lately either. I'll just have to wait and see what I can scrounge up when we dock at Little Rock."

That night a severe winter storm descended on the little towboat and he had to forget about Mother's Comfort. The frenzied winds made the fire pots hiss and sputter, and drove the sleet sideways against the cabin doors and deep into the bulkheads. The water became so rough that, even with guide ropes, only the most seasoned hands could move about. When the captain decided that it was too dangerous to put into Little Rock, he ordered the anchor dropped just outside the channel.

All night long, as they rode out the storm, the wind howled like a banshee, frightening children and grownups alike. The noise was dreadful but even worse for Ben was the sound of his fellow passengers calling for help as they moaned and retched. He was so seasick himself that he could do nothing to help.

He lay there, throwing up yellow bile into his blue bandanna, and then when there was nothing more to bring up, gagging over and over with the dry heaves. He longed for home, for Hettie, and for an end to this terrible journey.

The next morning the wind died down, and the violent rocking of the boat abated long enough for the *Victoria* to put into port. Towards noon, the Drew party was finally able to disembark.

The scene on the shore was grim. Several hundred souls, worn out from the storm-wracked voyage, huddled together for protection against the wind and chilling rains.

Quatie was among the last to start down the gangplank. She was deep in conversation with one of the crew who kept wanting to carry her. She was insisting that she could walk. Ben quickly strode back up onto the towboat and, without asking, took the liberty of lifting her up in his arms.

"Ma'am, you need to save your strength," he said firmly to her. "We still have a long way to go, you know."

She relented and allowed him to carry her to the wagon. He leaned in and set her down gently.

But he had no time to look for honey or lemon peel or anything else, because Conductor Drew was anxious to take advantage of what little daylight was left. As soon as the wagons were loaded up, the party set out.

For most of the afternoon, Ben, with Little Tuti at his side, marched beside Quatie's wagon. Even though it was wet and bitterly cold, the little girl did her best to match him stride for stride.

After an hour or so, he sensed that she was tiring. Reaching for her hand, he bent down to encourage her, and, as he did so, he noticed, for the first time, the crusted and peeling sores on her wrists. He was beginning to see a number of cases of this skin condition among the Cherokees, but, curiously, none at all among the crew of the *Victoria.*

When they reached Fort Gibson in Indian Territory, he definitely planned to ask Dr. Powell about this strange malady. He also wanted to know why the sores were only on the exposed areas of their bodies. He always thought the sun was supposed to heal, not make things worse.

His thoughts were interrupted when Tuti suddenly stumbled and went down on one knee. He picked her up in his arms and settled her against his chest. She put her arms around his neck and laid her head gratefully in the hollow of his neck. A short time later, she nodded off, and he turned towards the slowly moving wagon and carefully transferred her into Quatie's waiting arms.

Several hours later, the temperature began to drop even more and the rain turned back into sleet. Commander Drew decided to camp for the night on a high bluff just west of Little Rock even though they'd only covered a few miles.

After helping with the tents, the cooking fires, and the distribution of the provisions, Ben made his final rounds of the day, and then crawled, exhausted, into the escorts' tent. Pulling his overcoat tightly around him, he curled up on his side with his knees against his chest. He picked up a ragged old shawl someone had left there for him and pulled it over his head.

If only he could shut out the suffering around him along with the cold, he thought to himself. Besides worrying about Quatie and some of the others, including Tuti's father, he was also concerned because he was running low on many of his medicines. He'd given a list of the drugs and remedies he needed to Chief Ross who hoped to requisition the needed supplies in Little Rock. In fact, he was off right now trying to get help for the group.

After a long time, Ben was finally able to fall into a troubled sleep, but sometime during the night the screaming of the wind awakened him. When he opened the tent flap, his face was peppered with icy needles.

"We'd have done better staying on that boat until this storm died down," he muttered.

Worried about his patients, especially Quatie, he forced himself to get up to check on them. As he went from tent to tent, he found most of them lying quietly, and he did not disturb them.

But when he poked his head into Quatie's wagon, it was strangely silent. When he heard no rasping or strained breathing, he knew something was terribly wrong. He quickly reached over and set his lantern down on the floor inside and climbed in after it.

He saw Tuti first. She was sound asleep, wrapped in a heavy dark cloak. The hood was tied snugly around her sweet little face. He recognized that cloak. Now, he was afraid to turn around and look at Quatie.

She was lying there, dressed in her long sleeved brown dress with the high-necked brown and white ruffled collar. She was barely breathing. He quickly removed his own coat and placed it over her, but he knew in his heart that he was too late.

He called out for help. People awoke and came from all directions. They offered blankets and quilts that couldn't be spared, small pouches and tightly folded papers of precious herbs and ground roots, and even, in spite of all the wind and rain, some hot water to moisten her dry lips. Someone else quietly came forward and placed a folded saddle blanket under her head to ease the homeward journey.

The vigil began. Her family gathered around her, taking turns holding her hand, wiping her forehead, caressing her face, and speaking in low voices to her, and, finally, praying softly together. As the hours went by, her breathing became even more shallow and irregular. Each breath seemed to be the last until, finally, towards morning, Ben, waiting outside the wagon to give the family more privacy, heard the anguished and unmistakable sound of her death rattle.

In a way, he couldn't help but be relieved that it was over for her. She'd been sick for so long, and suffered so much. Yes, even though others might misunderstand, he'd have to say he was glad it was finally over.

"At least now she's found peace," he said softly, his voice breaking.

The storm was letting up. With the break in the weather, Ben knew the party would be pulling out in a few hours and they needed to bury her quickly. As word of her passing spread throughout the camp, many of the sorrowing Cherokees came forward again and offered to help with the interment.

Even though the ground was frozen and their tools makeshift, using the light from Ben's oil lantern and taking turns, they were able to complete the sorrowful task just before sunrise.

The makeshift grave they dug was shallow and muddy with slanted, uneven sides. There was no box to receive her body, and not even a shroud with which to wrap her.

On a bluff overlooking Little Rock, on February 1, 1839, with the soil from the grave mounded up on one side, the mourners quietly gathered alongside the trail and laid Quatie Ross to rest.

As they were filling in the last clods of dirt and then arranging the stones used to mark her resting place, the sun rose like it was any other day and streaked the sky with gaudy pinks and oranges.

And back in the wagon, the little girl slept on, warmed by the heavy dark cloak. The drawstring of the hood was still tied neatly in a bow under her chin, and in her scab-covered hand, she tightly clutched a crudely carved wooden bird.

Chapter 26

Home at Last

Lame Bear's farm
February 1839

At first, Hettie was just thankful and relieved to learn that her father was still alive after they'd given him up for dead and to learn that Halfmoon and Gertrude were safe too.

On the journey home from the cave, she and the other members of the little caravan picked their way slowly out of the mist-shrouded mountains. Sadie was so loaded down that she waddled unsteadily from side to side. The wheelbarrow, with Sky pushing it, was overflowing as well and the rest of them were struggling with bulging bales of precious belongings balanced precariously on their backs.

As she trudged along, Hettie was well aware that the boy with Halfmoon was the younger brother of the soldier named Benjamin Stone. Sensing her eyes on him, Gabriel who was leading the heavily laden mule, turned and smiled at her. It reminded her a little of his older brother's smile that time he'd showed up at their cabin just about a year ago to confiscate Lame Bear's rifle.

She remembered how their eyes had met and how he had smiled at her across the dark room while he waited in the doorway for the rifle; the time he'd spoken to her at the Council House in New Echota when she was learning to read and write. Then there had been that day in the cornfield when Mattie Poor had been out caning by the river. She had certainly noticed how friendly and warm he had been to Sky that day, laughing and joking with him. And how he had come right over to try to help her with the cane. Most of all, she reflected on the strange new feelings she had experienced when his hand had taken hold of her wrist. It all came rushing back.

But right now she was longing to see her father and Gertrude again, and she tried to focus her thoughts on to getting home.

"I don't feel like trying to sort it all out now, anyway," she decided. "Maybe later but not now."

During the evening, however, after the excitement of seeing Lame Bear and Gertrude and of being home had worn off, and after they had all shared Gertrude's bountiful meal of chestnut bread and baked sweet potatoes, she felt strangely unsatisfied and let down.

As she idly glanced around the cabin, she spotted Mattie Poor's sooty old soup kettle wedged forlornly in a corner of the fireplace. She pointed it out to the others.

"How come those Campbells, didn't throw that old soup kettle away along with everything else we owned?" she announced in a loud, irritable voice.

"After all, our hands were all over that too. Didn't that make it too dirty for them to want to use?" she asked sarcastically but got no response.

Some of their dappled blue and white enamelware, mostly the chipped and dented pieces, was left behind too, along with a few fireplace tools. But that was all.

She glanced around one last time looking in vain for her special dress or the little charcoal sketch the missionary's wife had given her, hoping. she'd overlooked them before.

But, thanks to Gertrude, every nook and cranny of the cabin was neat and tidy, and, except for a pile of sleeping mats, every well-swept corner was bare.

In place of Lame Bear's handmade furniture, Hettie disdainfully took in the motley assortment of barrels and wooden crates that Benjamin Stone had managed to scrounge up for them. She glanced up at Halfmoon and Gertrude's work aprons and shawls hanging neatly from the wall pegs where her petticoat, two dresses and linsey-woolsey smock should have been. She tried not to begrudge the old sisters the space, but, just the same, those used to be her pegs.

"Well, at least the place is clean, and warm even if all our things are missing," she decided, "and Lame Bear, he's getting well, and we're all safe, Halfmoon and Gertrude too.

"And, at long last, we're finally out of that smelly old cave."

But as she watched the four elders smiling and catching up with each other, she wondered why she felt so melancholy and left out.

"What's wrong with me, anyway?

"And look at Sky over there," she thought, "making friends with that white boy and settling in like he'd never been away."

Sky had laid out his marbles in front of the fireplace and was showing Gabriel how to play. As she observed the two boys, she wondered why she felt pangs of jealousy. She'd never seen any point to Sky's game before and avoided playing it herself if there was any way to get out of it, so why should she care now? But the fact was, she did.

She knew she was supposed to be grateful to the soldier, Benjamin, and this boy, Gabriel, for getting back their farm for them and for bringing Halfmoon and Gertrude here. But how could she forget that it was their kind who had stolen the farm and put the old sisters in that stockade in the first place?

It was all so confusing. After all, she and Sky had seen with their own eyes how Benjamin Stone had arrested Halfmoon and Gertrude, and now they were telling her that he had turned around and rescued them, snatched them right out of that emigration depot over in Tennessee. Halfmoon was even saying that Lieutenant Stone most likely had saved their lives because they'd probably have died on that trail like Chief Whitepath and all those others.

"I guess I'll have to give him that much," she thought grudgingly.

But the rest, about him liking her and all, and wanting to deed over the farm to her, well, she felt like those white folks owed them that much to begin with.

"And who said I have to like him back, anyway?"

Besides, how could she be sure he'd still care for her when he saw her again? She was a different person now, not the same girl she'd been before. She didn't look the same or, for that matter, feel the same either. He probably wouldn't want a tall skinny girl like her in the first place, she thought. She'd noticed that white men like him usually chose light-skinned Cherokees who acted ladylike and helpless.

"That's not me, and if he thinks I'm going to put on like that, he's got it all wrong. So there."

She got up and went to the corner to pick out a pallet. She carried it over to the space where her bed used to be and spread it out. But when she lay down, the mat felt all lumpy and scratchy, and smelled musty, besides. She missed the soft furs they'd left behind in the cave.

She tried several positions but none felt right. Finally, in frustration and anger, she flipped over onto her stomach and buried her head in her arms so that no one would see the tears that started to flow.

She cried about how close Lame Bear had come to dying, and about how cold and hungry they'd been for all those months. She cried about all the times she'd been afraid of getting lost while she and Sky were out hunting, especially after Lame Bear was gone, and she cried about the constant gnawing fear in her stomach all those months over being discovered.

"Would the Reservation really have been so bad? Was all that worry and fear worth it? Just to end up like this? What good does it do to be home again?" she asked herself.

"Everything's either burned up or stolen. And tonight Halfmoon was saying that even New Echota's a ghost town now, with everyone gone.

"What's the use?" she thought. "No matter what we do, it'll never be the same. No more Beloved Women, no missionary school, no Purification Festivals, not even those Green Corn Dances. All that's over forever.

"But I guess I should be thankful that at least we're safe now and not cold and hungry all the time like before. And we don't have to live in a cave anymore.

"So why am I feeling so miserable? Why can't I be like Sky and the others?"

Then she almost laughed out loud when it suddenly dawned on her that she'd never have to eat another one of Mattie Poor's bitter pot scrubbers as long as she lived!

"Now, there's something to be really thankful for," she thought, smiling through her tears.

She turned her head to the side and glanced over, wistfully, towards the fireplace. Sky and Gabriel had their heads together over the marbles, and the firelight was reflecting off Sky's handsome face. Gertrude was standing next to them, banking the fire for the night, and the others were getting out their pallets and deciding where to sleep.

A few minutes later, Hettie sensed movement behind her back. It was Mattie Poor, breathing hard, as she dragged her bedding over to where Hettie was lying. She heard the painful cracking of her grandmother's knees as she squatted down to spread out the mat. Hettie started to turn over to help her but then stopped because she was ashamed of her tears.

Mattie Poor, muttering softly to herself, was finally satisfied that the pallet was spread out just right. Hettie lay still and listened to the familiar sounds of her grandmother turning this way and that, like an old dog trying to find the best sleeping position.

Then, when all was quiet, Hettie felt Mattie Poor lean over and place her hand on her shoulder.

She reached around and clasped the dear old hand in hers. It felt knobby and coarse but she cradled it lovingly. She drew it over her shoulder and placed it against her wet cheek. Still holding tight, she sighed deeply and closed her eyes. Maybe tomorrow would be a better day.

CHAPTER 27

SONNY

Fort Gibson
(At the end of The Trail of Tears)
Spring 1839

As he had every morning since arriving five days ago at Fort Gibson, his final destination in Indian Territory, Ben checked for Sonny in all the stables on the grounds of the Fort, including the main stables bordering the lower vegetable gardens, the stalls up on the hill near the warehouses, the smaller ones behind the long commissary storehouse, and even the barns for the oxen down below on the bottom land next to the Neosho River.

Each day, he hoped that somehow he'd overlooked Sonny the time before or that someone had brought him in during the night.

There was an atmosphere of utter confusion at the Fort. Ben was concerned that the high turnover of personnel and animals could make it easy to overlook a single horse. Even one as special as Sonny.

He scoured every detachment list for Dr. Powell's name and every inventory for a horse of Sonny's description. He inquired at the hospital, the commandant's office, the barracks, and in the officers' and the enlisted men's messes. Several times a day he'd made the rounds of all the wells and cisterns that dotted the hilly grounds around the fort, paying special attention to the ones where he'd noticed that newcomers were apt to water their animals. But there were no answers for him. No one knew Dr. Powell and no one had seen a horse like Sonny.

Unfortunately, he knew that many of the incoming Indians had already passed through the Fort and then departed for the homes of friends and relatives or to plots of land assigned to them. The last two removal parties, headed by Hildebrand and Taylor, had reached the Fort earlier in the week, and, as far as anybody knew, there were no more Cherokees still out on the trail.

He grew discouraged but then he hadn't expected it to be easy. He never gave up hope that eventually he'd find somebody who knew where Sonny was or at least could tell him what happened to him.

Ben spent hours laboriously hand lettering and then tacking up tag board signs in the barracks, the mess halls, even the dispensary, asking for information about Dr. Powell's whereabouts, and offering a reward for Sonny's return. He asked about them everywhere he went and was constantly nagged by the thought that it might be too late. For all he knew, someone had already walked off with Sonny.

He had other pressing concerns too. He'd just learned that little Tuti's father was dead, that he'd expired two days after they'd reached Fort Gibson.

"She's just a babe and already she's had to face death so many times," he thought.

"Probably even more than I know about, because, most likely, she lost her own mother too."

Someone told him other Cherokees had taken her in, as was the Nation's custom, but now these people were getting ready to move on to a place called Park Hill and were looking for another family to adopt her.

He needed to find her, if only to give her new family a supply of the salve he had taught her father to put on the sores on her wrists. He also wanted to make sure they knew to feed her bread and meat as well as the corn that all the Cherokees were so fond of.

A doctor stationed at the Fort's dispensary had told him that too much cornmeal might be the cause of the strange skin malady afflicting the Cherokees. Now, he wanted to make sure that whoever took in the little girl would understand the need for other kinds of food for her.

Ben recalled evenings on the trail when he'd seen many of the Indians genuinely puzzled about what to do with their allotments of flour. Sometimes the whole ration had gone to waste.

He also wanted to make sure they'd find a good family for Tuti. He knew that back in Georgia the Cherokees had always provided for their own, even children whose parents died. He knew also that several years ago the Government had given the Cherokees already here on the Reservation enough money to build an orphan home but he didn't see how they'd be able to accommodate the growing number of new waifs orphaned by cholera, dysentery, tuberculosis, pneumonia and all the other diseases that had struck the Cherokees on the trail.

"Besides, what kind of life would a little girl like her have in an orphanage," he reasoned uneasily.

"She's such a timid little girl, she'd probably hide out like she did on the boat and hardly ever show herself, most likely not even get enough to eat. Who knows what could happen to her? And she's already been alone too much as it is."

He was starting back towards the office in the stockade to find out where she'd been taken and who had her now, when up on the knoll beyond the laundress houses, he spotted a familiar old figure slowly leading a horse out of the trees into the clearing and down the hill toward the Fort.

He leaned forward and squinted, trying for a better look as he impatiently brushed his unshorn hair out of his eyes.

"It isn't," he exclaimed! It can't be!"

"Jesse Birdsong! As I live and breathe!

"Is it really you?" he shouted at the top of his lungs, thumping his chest and leaping sideways towards them.

"And who's that with you?" he yelled, laughing wildly as he began to run up the hill.

"Is it really my Sonny? Yes, by God, it is. I can't believe it. It really is."

Sonny was already nickering at the sound of Ben's voice and Birdie was struggling to slow him down.

The two men met on a small plateau in the middle of the hill, solemnly shaking hands and exchanging greetings while Ben tried to calm down. Then Birdsong passed over the rope to him and Ben began to lovingly inspect his horse, first cupping Sonny's soft velvet muzzle between his hands while he checked his mouth, eyes, and ears. Then he ran the palms of his hands up and down his powerful shoulders and front legs and, finally, across his smooth withers.

Birdsong waited until he saw that Ben was finally satisfied his mount was sound before he began to speak.

"Old Doc Powell," he explained, "he passed on real sudden-like only a day or two after you and the Ross Party had left. It was just after we crossed into Illinois, I believe it was. They found him one morning, stone cold and stiff as a barn door. They said his tired old self was just plum wore out.

"You know, he should of been the one they sent on that towboat instead of you. He was too old and feeble to tolerate all that hardship.

"Afterwards, they used that big old bay of his to help pull the wagons and probably would of did the same with your Sonny, here, except I stepped up and maybe lied a little when I said you'd told me to care for him and see that you got him back when we reached Fort Gibson if anything happened to Doc Powell.

"Like Old Doc promised you," he added, solemnly.

"How'd you know about that?" Ben asked curiously. Birdie scratched his head and thought for a minute.

"Oh, you know how word gets around."

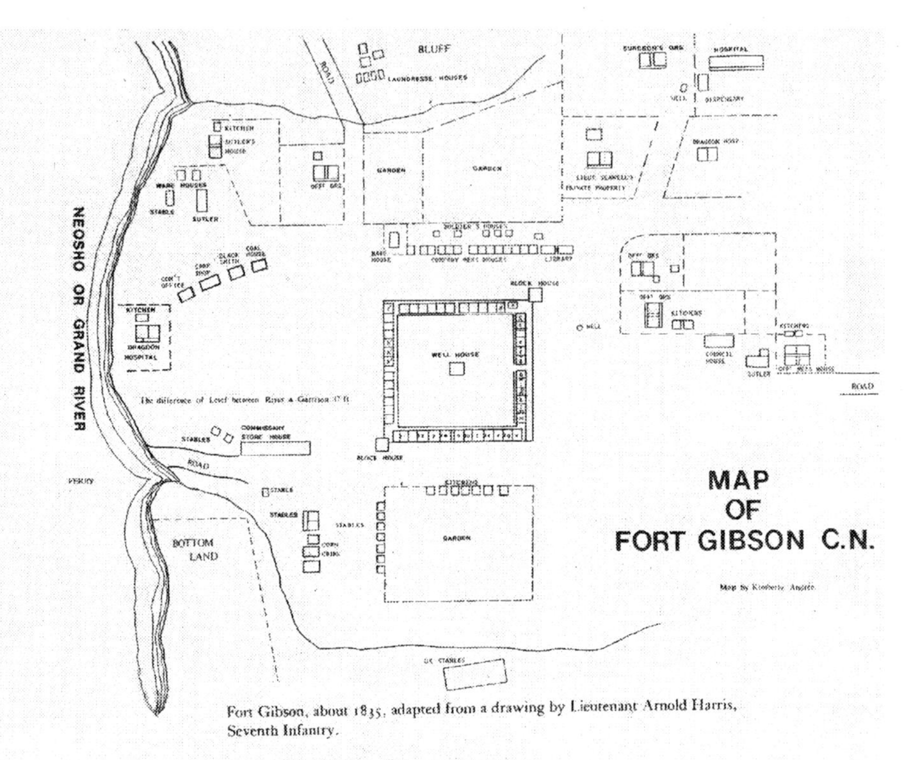

Fort Gibson, about 1835, adapted from a drawing by Lieutenant Arnold Harris, Seventh Infantry.

Key to Map 4, Fort Gibson about 1835:

-a — Magazine
-b — Acting Assistant Adjutant General's Office
-c — Officers' Quarters
e, f, g — Officers' Quarters, upper and lower room
h — Officers' Quarters, lower room, Quartermasters's Office
i, k, l, m — Officers' Quarters, lower room, Soldiers' Quarters
-o, q — Company Store Rooms
-p — Company Store Rooms, lower room, Soldiers' Quarters
r, s, t — Soldiers' Quarters
u, v, x, y — Officers' Quarters
-d', e' — Company Store Rooms
h' — Guard House and Cells
All the other rooms, Soldiers' Quarters

1835 Map of Fort Gibson

CHAPTER 28

TUTI

Ross's Landing, Tennessee
May 1839

"It won't be long now," Ben said to a weary Tuti who was riding on Sonny, leaning back against the lumpy saddlebags. The steamboat, *Mary Ann,* had let them out at Ross's Landing in Tennessee and they'd been traveling overland on their way to Ben's parent's farm outside of Dalton, Georgia.

The strong, almost cloying smell of roses hung heavy in the afternoon air. The sweet, sweet odor was overpowering and Ben thought the blossoms with their white daisy-like petals and bright yellow centers looked altogether different from any roses he'd ever seen before. They seemed to be popping up all along the worn trail, clinging to fences and stonewalls, nestling against the trees, and filling in many of the roadside clearings.

Last night they'd come across a Methodist circuit preacher on his way to his next service down in Calhoun. After introducing himself as the Reverend Horace Stringfellow, he had invited them to rest and share his campfire. When the pleasantries were over, Ben spoke about the profusion of roses all around them.

"Yes," the Reverend said. "Folks in these parts are calling them Cherokee Roses. The story goes that during the Army Removal last winter, everywhere a Cherokee mother shed tears, a new rose has now appeared in remembrance of her and her suffering."

He continued, "I don't know if it's true or not, but I can tell you, I've lived around these parts for nigh onto thirty years and I've never seen roses like these before."

Later, as was his habit each night before getting out their bedrolls and preparing to turn in, Ben gently rubbed his special salve into the rough skin on Tuti's hands and wrists. For the better part of two weeks, besides treating her with the ointment, he had made sure that every single day, depending on what was available, she ate some vegetables, bread, or meat along with her regular corn dishes. He thought her skin was beginning to look a little better.

After they'd been on the steamboat *Mary Ann* for a while, he noticed that she'd grown especially partial to the griddlecakes and sinkers served at breakfast. He knew, however, that given a choice, she'd still take her hominy grits in a minute. Probably always would. But that was all right with him.

"Just so long as she eats other things too," he said to himself.

The next day, as they made their way towards Dalton, he started wondering again how his parents were going to react when he showed up with this little girl. To say nothing of what Hettie would think. He couldn't even begin to imagine what her response would be.

"I guess I won't worry about that until the time comes," he decided. "Anyway, what's done is done and, besides, there's nothing I'd do any different even if I had it to do over."

Ben's parents had written him that Hettie had been found and was home now, living with the whole bunch: Lame Bear, Mattie Poor, Sky, Halfmoon, Gertrude and Gabriel, on the farm he had gotten back for them.

He was excited about the prospect of seeing her again and didn't plan to linger long at his folks' place.

"We'll spend just enough time at home for Maw and Paw to get to know you and to find out how Hettie is and how my brother Gabriel made out while I was gone," he explained to Tuti.

"Then I expect you and me, we'll be moving on to Lame Bear's place."

The Army had given him less than six weeks to report for his next assignment as a medic at Fort Butler in Murphy just across the Georgia border in North Carolina. The trip east had already used up almost three of those weeks.

He was pleased, though, that he'd be able to continue doctoring and at the same time be fairly close to home even if it wasn't in Georgia proper, but he wished he had more time to court Hettie as well as to prepare for his new post.

Just before he and Tuti had boarded the *Mary Ann* in Arkansas, he'd been able to make some small inroads into his lack of medical knowledge, although he would be the first to admit that he still had a long way to go.

They had been passing through Little Rock on their way to the docks and had gone into a dry goods store to buy bloomers, a shift, and a dress for Tuti to replace the threadbare clothing she was still wearing under her brown cape.

Afterwards, they had wandered down the shop-lined main street and eventually stumbled upon a second-hand bookstore on the corner. He was browsing leisurely through some dusty crates in the back looking for medical textbooks, when it suddenly dawned on him that maybe Tuti did not know how to read.

"Do you know any of these letters?" he asked her, pointing to the title page of a book. Embarrassed, she shook her head. He placed his hand on her shoulder.

"It's all right, Tuti," he said gently. "Lots of children your age haven't learned yet. And we're going to do something about it right now!"

He started searching in some of the boxes of children's books while she stood to one side, watching curiously. Soon, with a triumphant look on his face, he pulled out an old hornbook; its translucent pellucid cover had been half torn off, but otherwise it was in good condition. He also found a well-used slate for her to practice on.

And for himself, he picked out a dog-eared copy of *Dr. Brown's Pharmacopoeia.*

"Even I've heard of this old standby," he exclaimed happily as he handed his purchases to the clerk.

On board the *Mary Ann*, he and Tuti had quickly settled into a daily routine. Every morning after the sinkers and twisters, they set themselves up at a table on the main deck. While she patiently copied her capitals, he boned up on the best treatment for quinsy. And when she practiced her lower-case letters, he read up on leeches and blood letting. After going over the Lord's Prayer, her next exercise on the hornbook, he used old pieces of sinew to practice Dr. Brown's tried and true ligature tying techniques while she copied the prayer in her neat little hand. And then, in return for his help, she taught him how to recite the prayer in Cherokee.

By the end of the boat trip, Tuti had worked all the way down to the fancy Roman numerals on the last row of the hornbook, and he had managed to fill in some of the bigger gaps in his doctoring ability. Nevertheless, as soon as they got to Murphy, he planned to find a grammar school for her and more textbooks for himself.

Now, as they walked along, he picked up the pace to be sure they'd be home before dark. He hoped his father would still be working out in the fields so his mother could meet the little orphan girl first and help him break the news. He knew she'd be receptive to the sweet child, and besides she always took to new ideas better than his father.

"It's not going to be easy, though, trying to explain something I don't quite understand myself," he thought to himself.

Back at Fort Gibson when he'd found Tuti again, before the idea of bringing her back with him had even occurred to him, it seemed like it was out of his hands.

"It was like everything had already been decided. Like she was the one who had picked me out instead of the other way around."

He smiled at the memory. "What was I to do? She'd already found her way deep into my heart. I was hooked!

"Besides, even though, in the end, I couldn't save Quatie, there's no way I was going to miss out on the chance to help this little babe.

"But, boy, did I take a lot of ribbing around the officer's quarters for being such a soft touch. Whew!" he thought, "I'm sure glad we finally made it out of there!"

It was getting harder to see the road now and he began to walk even faster. Tuti, who'd been dozing, lurched suddenly in the saddle.

"Don't fall asleep on me now," he chided. "We want to get home before it gets any darker. Hang on tight!"

Soon, they made the final turn into the farm. He could see the warm yellow glow of an oil lamp in the farmhouse window at the end of the lane and could hear the familiar trill of the spring peepers in the damp woods beyond. As they got closer, he whistled the four singsong notes of his family's special call, and laughed out loud when, almost immediately, old Sadie answered him from the barn.

His mother, wiping her hands on her apron, appeared in the doorway of the farmhouse at the same moment that Gabriel and another young man, with a cow's horn on a rawhide string bobbing up and down on his chest, trotted around the corner of the barn.

"Hello, Maw," Ben called. "Hey Gabe. Who's that with you?"

"Oh, Ben, I can't believe you're home safe and sound. It's been so long," his mother said, embracing him.

"Don't you recognize this fellow?" Gabriel teased as he hugged Ben.

"Don't you know old Sky here, your honey's twin brother, for goodness sakes? I guess I should just be glad you can still recognize me, your own brother," he joked.

Ben extended his hand to Sky. "How do," he said, smiling.

Looking back at Gabriel, he asked, "What's with the cow's horn anyway?"

Gabriel said, "Maw was singing one morning last week, the day after Sky and me got back home to help with the spring planting, and she noticed that Sky seemed to pick up on some of the really high notes. She and Paw fixed him up with this here ear trumpet. If you yell real loud, he can hear you.

"Watch this!" he said, motioning for Sky to put the horn up to his ear.

"Hello Sky," he shouted into it.

Sky, grinning proudly, echoed back, "Lo Si."

"Who's that on Sonny?" his mother asked curiously.

"Her name's Tuti, Maw, and I'm her guardian. We were together over the winter on the trail west and then on the towboat with Chief Ross and his family from Paducah to Little Rock. After Tuti's father passed away, I guess she decided I was better than nobody at all, because she agreed to take her chances with me, and, well, here we are. Isn't that right, Tuti?"

He lifted her down from the saddle. Gabriel, with Sky at his side, took Sonny's reins and headed into the barn.

Taking Tuti by the hand, Ben stepped up to his mother who hesitated not at all before taking hold of her little hand and leading her towards the farmhouse.

"You hungry, child?" she asked. "Maybe we can find a little something to tide you over 'til supper. Must of known you was coming because I baked extra today."

Ben followed the boys into the barn and while they took off the tack and the saddlebags he loaded up a pitchfork with hay from the loft and began to fill the manger between Sadie and Sonny's stalls.

"All right," he finally said, "Don't keep me in suspense any longer! How's Hettie and what does she have to say about me? And what about Lame Bear and the others? They all right? Come on Boy, speak up. Tell me!"

"There's not much to tell, Ben," Gabriel, with a wink at Sky, drawled teasingly. Then he relented and began explaining.

"A couple of months back, me and Halfmoon and Gertrude were all together at that old folks home you stuck me in, when early one morning right in the middle of the worst blizzard of the winter, Lame Bear wandered back in. Half dead, he was, wrapped in old rags, and froze just about solid.

"Halfmoon and Gertrude worked him over pretty good before they brung him round. Later, even though he got patches of black rot, they managed to save most of his crooked old feet. Have you ever seen those things? He's still got his heels and a little more besides, but his toes is all gone.

"When Sky and I left to come here to help with the spring planting, the old man was just beginning to stand up and move around a little. I fixed him up with two walking sticks to lean on. Makes him looks like a giant daddy long-legs, if you ask me, but it works pretty good for him.

"After he was on the mend, Halfmoon left Gertrude to take care of him, and me and her took Sadie and headed up into the hills to fetch the others.

"Sky, here," he said, "just about scared the living daylights out of me, rising sudden like out of the grass by Turtle Rock like some ghost."

He threw his arms over his head and waved them wildly to make Sky laugh.

"Turned out, they was living in an old hunting cave, all skin and bones, getting by on Mattie Poor's dried pot scrubbers and whatever sorry game Hettie and Sky could bring in. They was mighty glad to see us, I can tell you, mighty glad.

"Now that Hettie's back home, she knows what you did for them, Ben, but I have to tell you, I overheard her telling Mattie Poor she can't never forgive you for taking away Lame Bear's rifle and then putting Halfmoon and Gertrude into that stockade over in New Echota besides."

Ben propped the pitchfork in the corner, straightened up, and took a deep breath.

"I know it's not going to be easy to win her over," he said, "but I've come this far and I'm not giving up now. I'll do whatever it takes. I'm not quitting. Not now, not ever."

As the darkness closed in, the three of them finished up in the barn and hurried across to the farmhouse.

CHAPTER 29

PLEADING HIS CASE

Lame Bear's farm
May 1839

Mattie Poor and Hettie were out in the cornfield, side by side, their long skirts tucked up into the waistbands of their aprons, tilling the soil around the evenly spaced bright green mounds of newly sprouting corn. Gertrude was trailing along behind them.

Every now and then she'd dip her hand into her apron pocket and pull out a fistful of squash seeds. Then she'd carefully open her palm and pick out exactly three seeds. Next, she'd bend over and with her stubby forefingers, push them gently into the newly softened warm earth and then use the heel of her hand to smooth over the surface.

Halfmoon was in the barn, helping Lame Bear put together a fish weir out of cane and willow. Moving around was still difficult for him, and his newly healed fingers were numb and stiff, but except for a slight tinge to the whites of his eyes, he had no traces of the bilious sickness that had plagued him in the cave, and his mind seemed clear again.

Ben's hands were sweaty and his stomach began to rumble ominously as he and Tuti, with Sonny on a lead just behind them, walked out of the woods and down the hill to the farm. He had rehearsed in his head many times what he planned to say to Hettie, but when he spotted her working in the field, he felt his heart begin to drum in his ears, and his fingers on Sonny's lead begin to tremble.

"This is it," he said softly to Tuti. "I'll probably only have this one chance to make my case and I was never much good with words to begin with. Gabriel was always better at these kinds of things than me." He took a deep breath. "But here goes.

"Morning Ma'am, Morning Sir," he called to Halfmoon and Lame Bear who were watching him from the barn door.

"How are you today? With your permission, Ma'am, Sir, I'm here to have a word with Hettie. I see her over yonder in the cornfield with her grandmother and," he stopped and looked again, "is that Gertrude there with her? Yes, I believe it is!

"This here's Tuti," he said. "We got to know each other on the towboat going west and when her father died just after we reached Fort Gibson in Indian Territory, I arranged to be her guardian. We came back on a steamboat, the *Mary Ann,* and in a few weeks we'll be heading to Fort Butler in North Carolina where I'm to be stationed as a medic.

"Sure glad to see you're up on your feet again, Sir," he said to Lame Bear. "Gabriel told me you almost lost your life in a terrible blizzard."

"That's right, Lieutenant," Lame Bear answered in his rough voice. "We've been expecting you." He said and then paused before adding.

"We're much obliged to you for helping Halfmoon and Gertrude and for getting this place back for us. We heard what you did."

Halfmoon came forward and put her hand on Tuti's shoulder.

"Welcome, little one. We're glad to have you. Lame Bear here is building a fish trap. You can help if you want by handing him the cane after I strip it."

Tuti was too shy to speak, but she nodded eagerly and started into the barn with them as Ben looped Sonny's reins around a branch, and loosened his girth. With his heart pounding in his chest, he began the long walk out to the cornfield.

"Surely they must have noticed me by now," he thought, but the three women gave no sign. As he got closer, however, Mattie Poor and Gertrude stopped working and started walking back towards the cabin, leaving Hettie alone. She had stopped hoeing also and was now leaning her elbow on the worn wooden handle watching him approach.

He brushed his hair out of his eyes and cleared his throat.

"Morning, Miss Hester," he called, smiling.

"How are you today?"

He cleared his throat again. He couldn't believe that this moment was finally here.

"I've waited so long for a chance to speak to you and now, for the life of me, I can't remember what I've practiced over and over," he stammered.

Please excuse me if I get mixed up," he said as he tried to ease some of the tension by bending over and running his fingers lightly along the shiny tips of the bright green stalks.

"Looks like a fine year for corn, doesn't it?" he said brightly.

Hettie studied his face. He had changed quite a bit since their last meeting. There were deep lines around his eyes and mouth that hadn't been there before. She noticed too the telltale remains of chilblains spidering along his cheeks. But his intense blue eyes were the same.

Right now, those eyes were focused on her, searching her face as he tried desperately to find a way to convey the feelings he was having so much trouble putting into words.

"I'm sure Halfmoon and Gertrude have told you that this place belongs to you now. I bought it back from the Campbells and gave Halfmoon the deed before I left for the west.

"I want you to know that no matter what happens between us, this place is still yours free and clear.

"Before I had to leave last winter," he continued, "I spent a lot of time trying to find you. I wanted to do whatever I could to help you and your family. I knew life up in those hills was going to be hard.

"I also wanted to tell you that I'm sorry for taking part in the roundup and to ask for your forgiveness. I was in the wrong. It wasn't until all those people were herded into the stockade at New Echota that I finally came to my senses, but by then it was too late."

He paused and then said, "I wish I hadn't done it."

He took a step closer and held out his hand. Taking a deep breath and closing his eyes for a moment, he said,

"Most of all, though, I wanted to let you know how much I care for you, Hettie. Do you remember that day in the cabin when you were sitting with your grandmother and I was standing in the doorway? I knew then that you were very special and that I wanted to be with you. I think that's when I first came to love you although I didn't realize it at the time."

His voice broke as he took a deep breath. "I'm so darned nervous I'll probably keel over right here and ruin everything."

He thought he detected the faint flicker of a smile across her face.

"Maybe it's too soon for me to be talking like this but I don't have much time. You know I'm an Army medic now and I have to report to Murphy in North Carolina in about three weeks. I wanted you to know where I stood before then.

"I hope you'll let me stay here until then so we can get to know each other better. That's all I'm asking Hettie, time to spend with you. That's all. I'm not out to rush you off your feet or anything like that.

"There's one more thing you need to know about me," he said, clearing his throat and hoping for the best.

"Did you see the little girl I got with me? Her name's Tuti, and she's Cherokee, like you. I met her on the way west. Her father was bad off with the coughing sickness and he passed on after the party reached Fort Gibson in Indian Territory. She's real shy and has no one else but me, far as I know. I'm her guardian now, all the kin she's got, just so you understand, she's my responsibility and, from now on, she'll be with me. She goes where I go."

He waited anxiously for her response. She seemed taller and thinner than the last time he'd seen her but she had the same serious demeanor as before. It was impossible for him to guess what she was thinking when, without a word, she abruptly turned away from him, took her hoe, and went back to work.

"So, what do you say, Miss Hester?" he asked in a quiet voice. "Can Tuti and I stay here with your family for a fortnight or so?"

When she didn't answer, he added, "Will you at least let us stay a few days? Can I ask your grandmother and your father for permission to stay?"

When there was still no response, he leaned down to retrieve Mattie Poor's hoe and began working alongside her, trying to match his strokes to hers. Every once in a while, however, when he had to bend over to untangle the weeds from his blade, he would fall behind. As he hurried to catch up, he caught her smiling at his clumsiness. His spirits rose.

Eventually, they heard the faint metallic clang of a wooden spoon being banged against a pot.

"That's Gertrude calling us in for the noonday meal," Hettie explained.

Side by side, they began to walk across the field. From time to time, their shoulders brushed against each other.

They leaned their hoes against the trunk of the old oak by the cabin and went to the well. He poured water from the ladle over her hands as she rubbed them together, and then dipped it again and passed it over to her to do the same for him. Instead, she placed the ladle back into the bucket and walked away.

Uncertainly, he followed her into the cabin. The others were already inside, seated on barrels and stools of uneven heights around the scarred and pitted plank table, their faces turned expectantly towards the door.

When Tuti caught sight of him, she jumped up and ran to him, taking him by the hand, and guiding him to a place beside her.

He sat down. Soon the others resumed their conversation. Both he and Gabriel had picked up a lot of Cherokee when they were growing up, and he had learned even more while he was on the trail, so he had little trouble making out what was being said. They were talking about planting crops. He listened carefully and waited politely for a lull.

"How about putting some rutabagas in with the corn and the squash later in the summer?" he suggested earnestly in his best Cherokee as he passed the cornbread. "That way, you can harvest them even after the first frost and well into the winter."

He heard a muffled snort at his elbow as Tuti suddenly doubled over, holding her hands over her face and shaking with silent laughter. Puzzled, he looked around.

"What's so funny?" he asked innocently, a little embarrassed.

No one answered and he began to feel slightly annoyed. He avoided Hettie's eyes and, instead, looked in vain for answers in the four grizzled old faces staring stoically back at him.

"Did I use the wrong word for rutabagas? What? Tell me!"

He turned to Hettie who was sitting across from him. He saw that she doing her best to keep a straight face.

"What's going on? What did I say?" he pleaded. "Won't somebody tell me?"

Hettie finally spoke up. "What you said was, 'How about planting some duck feathers in with the squash and the corn.'

"What are you planning to grow anyway?" she giggled. "Eider down pillows?"

Now, even Ben had to laugh.

After the meal ended, Lame Bear quietly hobbled over and invited him to spend some time in the *osi* when the day's work was done. Towards this end, before he went back to hoeing with Hettie, Ben lugged logs and some kindling from the woodpile and placed them on the ground next to the fire-ring outside the lopsided east-facing steam hut.

His heart was full of hope as he picked up the hoe and headed back out to finish reworking the soil for the squash seeds.

The Lord's Prayer

Pronunciation in the Cherokee Language

o-gi-do-da ga-lv-la-di-he-hi
Our Father, heaven dweller,

ga-lv-quo-di-yu ge-se-s-di de-tsa-do-v-i
My loving will be (to) Thy name,

tsa-gv-wi-yu-hi ge-sv wi-ga-na-nu-go-i
Your Lordship let it make its appearance.

a-ni-e-lo-hi wi-tsi-ga-li-s-da ha-da-nv-te-s-gv-i
Here upon earth let happen what you think,

na-s-gi-ya ga-lv-la-di tsi-ni-ga-li-s-di-ha
The same as in heaven is done.

ni-da-do-da-qui-sv o-ga-li-s-da-yv-di s-gi-v-si go-hi-i-ga
Daily our food give to us this day.

di-ge-s-gi-v-si-quo-no de-s-gi-du-gv-i
Forgive us our debts,

na-s-gi-ya tsi-di-ga-yo-tsi-na-ho tso-tsi-du-gi
the same as we forgive our debtors,

a-le tla-s-di u-da-go-le-ye-di-yi ge-sv wi-di-s-gi-ya-ti-nv-s-ta-nv-gi
And do not temptation being lead us into,

s-gi-yu-da-le-s-ge-s-di-quo-s-gi-ni u-yo ge-sv-i
Deliver us from evil existing.

tsa-tse-li-ga-ye-no tsa-gv-wi-yu-hi ge-sv-i
For thine your Lordship is,

a-le tsa-li-ni-gi-di-yi ge-sv-i
And the power is,

a-le e-tsa-lv-quo-di-yu ge-sv ni-go-hi-lv-i
And the glory is forever.

e-men
Amen.

The Lord's Prayer in Cherokee

And then, in return for his help, Tuti taught Ben how to recite The Lord's Prayer in Cherokee.

CHAPTER 30

THE *OSI*

Lame Bear's farm
Later The Same Day

As the sun was beginning to go down, Ben and Hettie, more relaxed and at ease with each another, returned from the long afternoon spent hoeing the cornfield. They caught sight of wisps of smoke rising from the *osi* and smelled the fragrant odor of cedar. Ben noticed that the logs he had piled up were untouched, right where he'd left them, and next to them was a smaller, neater stack of dark, riven wood. It was then he realized that not just any wood would do. It had to be special.

"I've sure got a lot to learn," he thought to himself, wiping the sweat off his forehead with his blue bandanna.

"My father is ready for you," Hettie said with a shy smile before she continued on into the cabin.

Ben lifted the tattered canvas hanging across the entrance to the sweat lodge and peered in. He saw that Lame Bear already had his clothes off and was sitting cross-legged opposite the entrance.

"I've been waiting for you," he said as he poured a ladle of water onto the red-hot rocks he had rolled from the fire-ring outside into the center of the *osi*.

"Come in."

Ben disrobed, modestly cupped his hands over his genitals and, crouching low, gingerly sidestepped through the doorway. The rocks seemed to hiss a welcome as they sent up great clouds of steam. Lame Bear motioned for him to make a complete circle around them before sitting down.

Ben did as directed and then settled his bony buttocks onto the prickly bed of pine needles. He crossed his long legs as best he could.

At first the dense moist heat felt incredibly comforting and he surrendered himself totally to its allure. As it continued to thicken and swirl around him, however, it soon became oppressive until he felt like he was suffocating. He tried to breathe faster to compensate but each breath seemed more shallow and less satisfying than the last. He was embarrassed to tell Lame Bear that he was in trouble but he was close to panicking when Lame Bear finally spoke again.

In a deep, guttural voice, he said,

"Lay down over there next to the door and try not to fight against the grandfather rocks."

Ben did as he was told. There, as he lay gasping, curled up like an infant, he found a tiny draft of cool air seeping in under the canvas door. He sucked at it greedily. Temporarily sated, he forced himself to relax, slow his breathing, and get control of himself again. It was then he noticed that Lame Bear was waiting to speak again.

"This is what the old men told me when I was a boy," he said, gravely, with a deep grunt.

"These rocks represent our grandfathers, the brave hunters, who have gone before us. Here is what they say.

"The people are an honorable people; we have always trusted in the wisdom of our two leaders, the Red Chief of War, and the White Chief of Peace. Unless the Red Chief spoke, we kept the peace, first with the Iroquois, and then with the Choctaw, the Seminoles, the Chickasaws, and even the Creeks as well as with the white man. But, now, we no longer have the Red Chief and the White Chief. We have only the one Chief of the Council who speaks for us all but sadly, like our brothers and sisters, he has gone very far away.

"Today, all that is left of our Nation are the Cherokees who live over in Quallatown and those few of us just now coming out of the hills to reclaim the land that the Great Spirit *Galun'lati* gave to us. We are all that is left of the Principal People; even our Eternal Flame has been carried to the west.

"I am an old man now and my time on earth is short. I am grateful to you for returning our farm to us and for helping Halfmoon and Gertrude. Word has also spread among us about all you did last winter to save lives along those trails where our people cried. And now you have even taken the little Cherokee girl, Tuti, into your heart. You are a good man, Lieutenant.

"Therefore, as the old men have taught me, I am bringing you into the Cherokee Nation to live among us, for as long as you desire. With Hester at your side, if that is her wish and yours as well. If you accept, you will be one of the Principal People forever more."

Ben sat quietly, no longer struggling for air, listening to all that Lame Bear was saying. He felt humbled by the words. At first he was so overcome, he couldn't speak. Finally, however, after composing himself, he found the words he needed.

"Sir, I humbly accept this great honor. I will work hard to care for the people and the land as you have done and I will always protect my daughter Tuti, and Hester, if she will have me. I promise you, Sir, at this, the most solemn moment in my life, I will never let you down. You have my word on it."

That night, after a final ritual bath in the river, feeling incredibly clean and at peace with himself, Ben entered the cabin looking for Hettie, hoping she was still awake.

Instead, he found her sound asleep, curled up on her pallet, with her arms wrapped protectively around the little girl. He was overwhelmed by the love he felt for them both and tears welled up in his eyes as he stood looking down at the two sleeping forms.

He carefully let himself down behind her and fitted his body lightly against hers. He took his hand and slowly brushed the long, silky hair out of her face. She stirred and he felt the sudden tenseness in her body as she realized who was there. He continued to stroke her hair as he whispered.

"You are the love of my life, Hettie, the only girl I have ever loved. There's no one else for me—not now—not ever. If you say no to me, I will go away, but it will break my heart. I will never stop loving you and thinking about you."

He took the middle finger of his hand and began to lightly trace a pattern around the outer rim of her ear. As he spoke, he made the circle smaller and smaller and then gently placed the soft pad on the tip of his finger directly over the opening in her ear. She stiffened slightly and her very small movement sent an overwhelming wave of desire surging through his body.

She turned over and used her backside to gently but firmly nudge Tuti's sleeping form over onto her own pallet to make room for Ben. Then she took hold of his hand and kissed each of his fingertips.

"I love you Benjamin Stone," she whispered.

Chapter 31

Loose Ends

The Stones' farm, Dalton, Georgia May 25, 1839

Sonny, pulling the lead wagon, led the small procession from Maw and Paw Stone's farm along the long winding road towards Lame Bear's place past Ellijay. The animal was clearly unhappy and doing his best to make sure Ben knew about it. He snorted and tossed his head from side to side and swatted at the gleaming new buckboard with contemptuous flicks of his tail. When those actions brought no results, he shivered his flanks under the unfamiliar long wagon reins and stamped his feet.

The indignity of a cavalry horse pulling a lowly wagon, even a new one, was just too much for him. To make matters worse, Ben and his father had hitched up another animal at the back. And it wasn't even Sadie. It was some new young mule, and, as far as Sonny was concerned, the last straw.

Ben was in the driver's seat doing his best to ignore Sonny's complaining. Mattie Poor was sitting primly beside him as they led the way back up into the heavily misted foothills of the Great Smoky Mountains. On her lap, she cradled a large oval pasteboard box whose lid creaked each time the shiny new metal clad wheels of the wagon went over a bump.

Mattie Poor hadn't mentioned the bandbox to Ben, and he hadn't asked, but in Dalton earlier in the day, while he and his father were dickering for the mule, he'd seen her in deep conversation with the proprietor of the dry goods store. And now she no longer had the double woven lightening basket she'd brought from home this morning. He wondered what she'd done with it.

Gabriel and Sky, full and drowsy from Maw's late afternoon meal of chicken and dumplings, were comfortably ensconced on a bed of blankets in the back of the new wagon keeping an eye on the skittish young mule.

Behind them, Maw and Paw, done up in their Sunday best, sat sedately in the family's old buckboard with Sadie in her familiar position at the helm. Every now and then she'd whinny at Sonny and he'd nicker softly back. The new mule would perk up his long pointed ears and look around. One of the boys would give a quick tug or two on the guide rope and Gabriel would cluck loudly until the frisky animal got back to business.

It had already been a long day. Ben and Mattie Poor had set off for Dalton before sunrise with Mattie Poor riding on Sonny's back and Ben walking alongside. In her hands, she clutched her new double lightening basket, the first she'd made since returning from the cave.

Ben had naturally expected that Hettie would be the one to go with him to Dalton. He wanted her to meet his parents and share with them the news of their upcoming marriage. Besides, he also wanted her help in picking out the mule and buckboard, his gift to her family at the blanket joining ceremony set for the next day.

But painful thoughts of unpleasant encounters with whites remained buried deep somewhere in Hettie's memory.

"It's better if you tell them first by yourself," she explained to Ben, "so they'll have time to get used to the idea of us being together."

"But they already know how I feel about you," he protested. "They know you're the only one for me and, besides, how could they help but love you?"

"Not all white people are like you, Ben," she said quietly. "It's really best this way. And be sure you let them know, we're having an English wedding too once we're settled in Murphy. Just in case that's worrying them.

"And while you're gone, my father and I can finish cleaning out the barn so you men'll have a place to sleep."

Mattie Poor had surprised him then by asking to go to Dalton in Hettie's place. Ever since they learned about the blanket joining, she, Halfmoon, and Gertrude had been seen more than once with their heads together. Something was afoot, and somehow it involved a trip to Dalton.

The unlikely pair had stopped first at Maw and Paw's before heading on into Dalton itself. Mattie Poor had been reluctant to dismount at the farm and Ben hadn't pushed her. Instead, he'd gotten his mother to come out to the barn so he could at least introduce them.

Ever gracious, Maw had invited the stubborn old woman to come inside for tea and biscuits, but Mattie Poor had remained in the saddle, saying,

"Thank you kindly, Ma'am, but we're on our way into town right now. Perhaps later on, before we head back home if that's agreeable with you."

"Yes, indeed," said Ben's mother, cheerily. "By then I'll have an early supper ready for us all. And, by the way, Jacob and me, we surely do appreciate your invitation to the blanket joining ceremony.

She went on, "I'm sorry Sky and Gabriel aren't back yet. They've been out squirrel hunting since early this morning. They should be back by now. You sure you don't want to come in and wait a spell?"

Mattie Poor replied, "Thank you, no, I've much to do in Dalton. We need to be on our way." She paused, looked at Ben, and then added,

"Ben here's told us how you discovered Sky could still hear some and then even fixed him up with an ear trumpet. We're much obliged."

Maw said, "We feel that God was working through us that day and we were just the messengers. But you should see him! He's learning new words every day and even beginning to say a word or two on his own. Truly, it is a miracle."

"That's for sure, it's a blessing all right." Mattie Poor replied.

Meanwhile back at Lame Bear's place, even with Mattie Poor and Ben gone, the cabin seemed too small and much too hot from all the cooking and other activities going on. Tuti, ordinarily mannerly and quiet, was underfoot so much that even placid and easy-going old Gertrude had to complain.

Besides, in addition to Tuti, she was having trouble fending off Halfmoon, her very own sister, who was getting more and more insistent about what should be included in the blanket joining rituals.

Lame Bear and Hettie had wisely retreated to the barn and were keeping busy picking up and throwing out. Hettie thought the space seemed too small for so many people until Lame Bear suggested he and Sky would probably sleep in the *osi* tonight.

"Ben, too, if he wants," he said.

Hettie was looking forward to having Sky home again and seeing for herself this hearing ability everyone was so excited about. She remembered last spring, when they first arrived at the cave, how he had reacted to the high-pitched noise of the bats. She should have followed up that day. A whole year had been wasted. Now, with her away, it would be up to the others to teach him. She wished she could bring him to Murphy with them, but she realized that he was needed here at home.

Her thoughts turned to Ben's parents.

She wondered if they would ever be able to accept her Cherokee ways. Would they turn up their noses at the way they lived, especially now when they had so little?

The waiting was stressful, and she was glad to be kept busy by Lame Bear who had perched himself on a wooden crate in the center of the barn and was giving orders right and left.

Finally, just as the sun was settling onto the jagged ridges of the mountains, turning them from their usual pale lavender into a deep smoldering purple, she heard the jingling of the harnesses and the crunching of the wagon wheels as the little group emerged from the woods and proceeded down the trace towards the barn.

Sky was so excited to see her that he jumped off the back of the rolling wagon, startling the new mule. After stopping to calm him, he ran to her, holding her tight as they rocked back and forth.

In their special sign language she told him that she'd missed him. Then she asked if he knew that she and Ben were to be married. He nodded his head yes, and then took a deep breath.

"Tea-ah, Tea-ah, Tea-ah," he said, pronouncing her name in a thick voice. She had never heard anything so beautiful.

"Oh, Sky," she said, gazing at him and lightly stroking his cheek before she turned away to welcome Ben's parents.

CHAPTER 32

THE BLANKET JOINING

Lame Bear's farm
May 26, 1839

The clouds were clinging stubbornly to the deep lavender mountains in the distance but the misty grayness of the morning was beginning to burn off the nearby foothills. Gertrude, Halfmoon, and Mrs. Stone were standing anxiously by the fire-ring waiting for Mattie Poor and Hettie who were still inside the cabin. The men, in their best clothes, were gathered awkwardly around the well. Ben, with Tuti at his side, was wondering why Hettie was taking so long. He hoped she wasn't going to change her mind.

His mother had done her best with his Sunday suit but even though he was thinner than when he wore it last, he had grown taller and more muscular. She'd let down both the sleeves of his jacket and the cuffs on the trousers as much as she possibly could, but, still, it didn't fit right. He kept tugging at the ends of the sleeves trying unsuccessfully to cover his wrists. He hoped Hettie wouldn't notice.

Suddenly, the cabin door opened and Mattie Poor emerged with Hettie directly behind her. For just an instant, Hettie stood poised in the doorway before stepping carefully out onto the ground. Ben was stunned. She looked just like a princess from a book of make-believe.

He knew, as soon as he saw Hettie's dress, why Mattie Poor had insisted on going with him to Dalton. Shaking his head, he wondered how many more double woven lightening baskets she'd had to promise to make for the shopkeeper and how long it would take her to pay off what she must owe for a dress like this.

It was made of alternating rows of white dotted swiss and sky blue satin ribbon. The high collar was banded in the ribbon and edged with white ruching. The long leg-of-mutton sleeves puffed out from Hettie's shoulders like angel wings and then tapered down into narrow blue satin cuffs held in place at her wrists with tiny pearl buttons. The fitted bodice accentuated and modestly drew attention to her beautiful breasts. The skirt billowed out from the stylish wasp waist and cascaded around her in frothy layers.

All eyes were on her as she took her place in front of the oak tree and motioned for Ben, who had been standing there gaping, to come and join her. The others, except for the Stones, came forward and joined hands, forming a ring around them.

Lame Bear broke the silence with the plaintive notes of a Cherokee song as he shook his special turtle shell rattle and chanted out the words. The group began a slow, heel-to-toe dance. When they had circled the couple seven times, they raised their arms to the Great Spirit and came together.

Then, Mattie Poor picked up the *selu*, the special dried ear of corn, which Halfmoon and Gertrude had chosen for the ceremony, and held it high over her head as she addressed the gathering.

"We give thanks to you, Oh Great Spirit, for the Mother Earth beneath us and the Sky Vault above us," she said. "The spirit of the eagle is with us today as we celebrate the joining of the blankets of Hester of the *Ani-Gatogewi*, or the Wild Potato Clan, and Benjamin who has no clan of his own.

"Now they will walk together instead of alone within the Universal Circle of Life that includes the four hills of life: infancy, childhood, adulthood, and old age."

She passed the ear of corn to Lame Bear who had propped himself against the oak tree to spare his feet. After he received the corn, he stepped away from the tree and stood on his own.

Gazing off into the distance, he intoned in a deep, guttural voice, "This is what the old men told me when I was a boy."

Then he turned to Hettie and Ben and spoke directly to them.

"Everything has a place in our way of life. With this joining of blankets comes a special responsibility for you, Hester, and for you, Benjamin, to respect not only each other, but also all those who have gone before, and all those who will come after.

"Like all the people, you have a special responsibility to care for our land and all living things that dwell on it."

He handed the *selu* to Halfmoon and leaned back again into the support of the tree.

Halfmoon, after accepting the corn, began to speak.

"The Eternal Flame, which is the center of our Circle of Life, was given to us long ago by the Great Spirit *Galun'lati*. Sadly, it no longer burns here, because last winter our people were forced to leave our lands, and they carried it away with them.

"But remember, even though the Eternal Flame is no longer here, the spirit of the Flame will always linger in our hearts."

Gertrude took the *selu* next and turned towards the couple with a smile on her kindly old face.

"May you always walk safely and wisely on the path within the Circle of Life," she began, speaking so softly the Stone family had to lean forward to catch her words.

"May the Great Spirit in the heavens continue to guide you but also you must remember to keep your feet planted on Mother Earth so that she may protect you as we protect her."

Next she leaned down and picked up their nicest Army blanket, which was folded neatly on the ground beside the couple. Halfmoon joined her and together they stepped forward and with wide, sweeping movements, solemnly placed the blanket around the shoulders of the couple who each took a corner of the blanket and drew it closer around them. Then Gertrude solemnly pressed the ear of corn or *selu* into Hettie's free hand.

Hettie turned towards Ben and looked into his eyes.

"Benjamin Stone," she said softly, "this ear of corn represents my commitment to you. It is a token of the new beginning for us and a reminder of the heritage of our people and our Clan."

"Hester," he answered, as he held out his hand to receive the corn. "I accept this ear of corn as a token of our new life together."

Placing it under his arm, he reached into his vest pocket with his free hand.

"In return for this token," he continued, "I give you the Lieutenant bars from my uniform to symbolize my promise to you that I will always take care of you.

"Furthermore, I pledge to work for the betterment of your people who are now my people as well and finally I promise to love you with all of my heart until we are parted by death."

The group closed the ceremony with the traditional Green Corn Dance. Again, Lame Bear called out the beat while the others performed a slow, rhythmic dance in which they alternated movements of bending their knees to plant hills of corn and raising up on their tiptoes to pick the ripe, tasseled-out ears. Little Tuti came last, crouching low as she followed the others and pretended to drizzle corn-meal from her fingertips as she did her best to keep in step.

Afterwards, Ben and Hettie clearly relieved that it was over and all had gone well, stood together to accept congratulations. The hazy sunlight filtered down through the leaves of the old tree onto their young faces.

Ben's parents were the first to approach.

"Welcome to our family, daughter," Maw said, pressing her cheek to Hettie's. "You are a beautiful bride."

"Yes," said Paw, heartily. "Welcome to our family." He leaned over to kiss her forehead and then straightened up to shake Ben's hand.

"Congratulations, Son," he said.

Gabriel was hanging back, fidgeting as he impatiently waited his turn. His arms were wrapped around a large, colorful bundle. As the others watched curiously, he moved forward and presented it to Hettie.

"Here, Sister," he said dramatically.

"Maw wanted you to have this old quilt. Our Grandma made it a long time ago."

He looked over at his mother and then back at Hettie.

"I tried to tell her you wouldn't want this old thing, but she wouldn't listen. Besides, now, how am I supposed to get to sleep at night without it?" he joked. "But, anyway, here it is."

Hettie took it lovingly and touched her face to its folds.

"Mother Stone, this is a wonderful gift," she said. "Ben has told me so much about his special grandmother and what she meant to him. Thank you too for accepting me into your family.

"I will cherish this quilt and do my best to make you proud of me."

"O.K.," shouted Gabriel, feeling right at home. "That's enough speeches for one day! Come on, you all! Let's eat."

Later in the day, after all the excitement had died down and the Stones had left for home, Hettie reluctantly changed out of her dress. She busied herself helping with the rest of the cleanup and then she and Ben began to make preparations for their early morning departure with Tuti to Murphy.

Finally, when the evening dampness was beginning to settle over the land, Ben and Hettie, satisfied at last that most of the work was done, stood with Mattie Poor in front of the cabin and looked out together over the darkening mountains.

After a moment, the Beloved Woman spoke.

"Let me tell you one thing," she began, in her usual way.

"Today I have seen that even though most of our people have been driven out, there are still enough of us left, counting the ones over in Quallatown, to keep our ways alive for those who come after.

"Someday, we will be many again. We will be known as the Cherokees of the East and our people will once more walk unto these hills."

The End

Coming Home

On the journey home from the cave, the members of the little caravan slowly picked their way out of the mist-shrouded mountains.

0-595-31483-X